CW00506950

PLENTY OF C]

Plenty, FL 6

Lara Valentine

MENAGE EVERLASTING

Siren Publishing, Inc.
www.SirenPublishing.com

A SIREN PUBLISHING BOOK
IMPRINT: Ménage Everlasting

PLENTY OF CHANCES
Copyright © 2014 by Lara Valentine

ISBN: 978-1-62741-201-8

First Printing: May 2014

Cover design by Les Byerley
All art and logo copyright © 2014 by Siren Publishing, Inc.

Printed in the U.S.A.

PUBLISHER
Siren Publishing, Inc.
www.SirenPublishing.com

PLENTY OF CHANCES

Plenty, FL 6

LARA VALENTINE

Chapter One

Samantha James walked slowly down the hospital hallway, memories crowding her brain and making her head hurt. She hated hospitals. Her mother had died in this same building, although on another floor. It looked and smelled the same as it had when she was thirteen. The fact that she was almost thirty didn't seem to matter. She still felt tiny and powerless here. The fact was, lately, she felt tiny and powerless all the time.

She straightened her shoulders as she approached room 507. She was going to get a tongue lashing from her grandmother so she might as well get it over with. She pushed open the door and let her gaze scan the room. Her grandmother was the only person inside, the second bed empty, reading a magazine. Gran's sharp eyes immediately zeroed in on her and Sam felt a rush of emotion squeezing her chest.

Her grandmother dropped the magazine in her lap and beckoned. "Come here, child. It's about time you showed up. Where in the Sam Hill have you been keeping yourself?"

Samantha couldn't stop her smile. That was her Gran. Sam had always admired her grandmother's strength, her indomitable spirit. Part of her had been expecting a frail, old woman. She'd been afraid she might be too late.

Her steps quickened until she was folded in her grandmother's arms. Despite being in the hospital, her grandmother still smelled of lavender and baking bread. Sam wasn't sure how it was possible but it made her feel like a kid again.

"I've missed you, Gran. Are you okay? Are they feeding you in here? I just got the message this morning."

Gran patted the bed with a smile. "Sit. You ask so many questions. Age before beauty. I have questions of my own."

Sam wasn't sure she wanted to answer them, but knew Gran wouldn't give up until she found out what she wanted. Sam settled herself on the side of the bed, holding her grandmother's hand.

"I just got the message this morning. Lacey got a hold of me."

Lacey Carrington was Sam's ex-boyfriend's sister. One of them anyway. Sam had lost touch with most people in Plenty, but Lacey had made sure to stay in touch no matter what. Lacey was the kind of person who made friends for life.

Gran nodded. "She's a sweet one. You didn't get the message I left on your phone?"

Sam shifted her gaze to the window where the afternoon sun was streaming in. "I lost my phone and haven't had a chance to get a new one. Lacey called my work and left a message."

Sam's boss hadn't been very happy about taking a personal message but Sam hated her boss. He'd also expressed his extreme unhappiness about her taking time off to see her grandmother but she didn't care. Gran came first. Always. It was a shitty job anyway. Another in a long line of crap jobs she'd had in the last two years.

"So what exactly happened? Lacey said you fell."

Gran pushed herself up higher on the pillows wincing a little. "I did fall. Damn carpet was loose on the stairs. Fell ass over tea kettle."

"Gran, that's awful." Recrimination twisted Sam's guts. She should have been there taking care of her grandmother. A terrible thought occurred to her. "How long did you lie there before someone found you?"

Gran waved her hand. "Not long. Gabe came by to check on me shortly after. He or Jason come by every single day. They say it's to make sure I'm okay, but I think they just want some of my cooking. You know peach cobbler was always Gabe's favorite."

Sam stiffened in shock at hearing their names. She'd loved Gabe Holt and Jason Carrington since the day she'd turned twenty-one and they'd bought her a drink at the local watering hole. They'd been inseparable after that night. Until Jason and Gabe went to war, that is. Then everything had gone to hell. What she'd done hadn't helped things.

She tried to school her features so she wouldn't reveal her shock. "That's good he came by. That's good. I didn't know he was back."

At Sam's request, Lacey never mentioned Jason and Gabe after she had delivered the news Gabe had left town a little over two years ago.

"I came back last spring."

Sam closed her eyes and swallowed hard. His voice could still send shivers down her spine. She turned slowly, trying to keep a rein on the rush of emotions she was feeling. She'd hoped to have time to prepare before seeing either Gabe or Jason. Time to harden her heart and remind herself of everything that happened.

It was like the time apart fell away as she looked at them. Gabe and Jason were standing so close she could have reached out and touched them. She had to clench her fists to keep from doing just that. She cursed whatever deity was listening that the months and years apart had barely touched them. Jason was still tall, dark and handsome, his shoulders a mile wide in his deputy uniform and his stomach flat and taut. Gabe was no less handsome. If anything, he was better looking than she remembered. His golden brown hair caught the sun, his skin tan. He looked more muscular than in the past, his T-shirt straining at the seams to contain his biceps.

It was his eyes that caught her attention. When she'd last seen him, they'd been dark and cold, almost flat. Today, they were a warm gold-brown and full of life. She found herself lost in his gaze for a long moment and had to drag her attention away.

"Welcome back." Her voice sounded weak but she was proud of herself for being able to say anything at all.

Gabe brushed past her and leaned down to kiss Gran's weathered cheek. Samantha's entire body trembled as his manly scent wafted around her reminding her of the woods after a summer rain. She remembered when the three of them had gone camping and it had rained the entire weekend. They'd stayed in the tent the whole time, making love and talking about the future.

"Welcome back yourself." He smiled at her but turned back to her grandmother. "How's our best girl today? We brought you some food."

Gran's face lit up as Jason also pecked her cheek and started pulling Styrofoam containers out of a heavy brown bag.

"I'm starving. The food here is terrible, you know."

Sami twisted the strap to her handbag between her fingers. She wasn't ready for this. She wasn't sure she ever would be.

"I guess I should be going. I'll come again in the morning to visit you, Gran."

Her grandmother put her fork down and frowned. "You just got here. We haven't had a chance to catch up. I want you to tell me what you've been doing lately."

She felt three sets of eyes on her. "Working. Just working. You know how it is."

Jason smiled kindly, obviously aware of her discomfort. He probably hadn't expected to see her either. She wondered if he had a girlfriend now. Her gaze went to his left hand and it was gold band free.

"I know how that is. Ryan's made some good hires though, so hopefully I can work some more reasonable hours."

"How is Ryan?" she asked, trying to sound normal.

Jason grinned and her heart skipped a beat. "Same old Ryan. He and Jack got married not long ago. Nice girl, Jillian, originally from Chicago."

"That's nice. Good."

They seemed to have run out of conversation since no one had the guts to talk about the eight hundred pound elephant in the room. She turned back to her grandmother.

"I really should go. I'll leave you to eat but I'll come back in the morning and we can have a nice long chat."

"Where were you planning to stay?"

Heat rushed into her cheeks. She didn't really know. She'd planned to call Lacey and had hoped for an offer of her couch. Sam couldn't afford one of the cabins by the lake. She'd barely had enough money for gas to get her here. She'd even worked the lunch shift today before she'd traveled so she would have some cash tips in her pocket.

"Can I crash at the house?"

Her grandmother had owned the only bed-and-breakfast in Plenty until about eighteen months ago when she'd been forced to close it. Gran simply wasn't energetic or strong enough to take care of it by herself. Sam had wanted to come back and help but her own life had been in too much turmoil.

"I'm afraid the house is being tented for termites. Maybe Gabe and Jason have room for you."

Gabe stepped forward. "You can stay with us. We have an extra room."

It was the very last place she wanted to be. Too many memories she didn't have the luxury of remembering.

"I'll just call Lacey—" she began, but Jason cut her off.

"Lacey is living back at home with my parents. We have lots of room. You can stay with us." His expression softened. "No strings attached. You can come and go as you please."

"There you go, Sami. You can stay with the boys. I'll know

you're safe there."

Sam would have laughed if she wasn't on the verge of crying. Gabe and Jason were so far from boys it wasn't funny. As for safe? She hadn't felt safe in a very long time. Too long to even remember how it felt. She finally nodded, too exhausted to argue. She was bone tired and wanted to sleep for a week.

"Okay. Thank you," she added belatedly. "Um, where do you live?"

Jason's eyes widened in surprise. "Samantha, things don't change that much in a small town." He leaned closer, the warmth emanating from his body. "Things are the same."

Her chest tightened painfully at his intimate tone. He couldn't mean he still felt the same. He'd had a little more than two years to find someone else. Jason, or Gabe for that matter, had never lacked for female admiration. She stepped back to clear her head.

"I think I still remember where that is." She tried to keep her words light as Jason removed a key from his keychain before handing it to her, their fingers brushing. She could practically feel the searing heat shoot up her arm and straight to regions more southerly. She was in a bad state.

"I have to go back to work and Gabe has to head to the club. Help yourself to anything in the kitchen and make yourself at home. You know, shower or whatever. You can have the blue-and-brown bedroom at the end of the hall."

Sami resisted the urge to smell her armpits. She'd showered in the morning but had worked a four hour shift before heading here so her aroma could be iffy. Jason was either trying to give her a big hint or just being a good host. Maybe both.

"Thanks, I'll head out then." She kissed Gran and gave her a big smile. "I'll be here in the morning, first thing. Sleep well, Gran."

Gran hugged her and patted her back like she did when Sami was a little girl and kids at school had teased and bullied her for not having parents.

"I'm glad you're back, child. It's time you were home."

Sami blinked back the tears she felt welling up. She didn't have the heart to tell her grandmother the truth.

She couldn't stay. She wouldn't bring trouble to Plenty and the people she loved.

As soon as Gran was better, she would be on the road again. A new town, a new job, maybe even a new name. What she needed was a new start and some luck.

* * * *

Jason's heart was beating like a marching band inside his chest. His sister had warned him she'd called Samantha, but he hadn't expected to see her so soon. She was as beautiful as he remembered, but she looked tired and sad. Her long blonde hair was still as golden and her blue eyes were still so vivid they were almost purple. But her skin didn't have the bloom he'd last on seen her. She'd looked thinner as well. Jason knew it was fashionable for women to be slim, but he'd always liked Sami's curves. He could remember nights he'd lost himself in her softness.

"You boys going to do right by my granddaughter this time?" Hazel Murray, known to everyone as Gran, shook her finger at him. "I don't want her leaving town with a broken heart. She damn near looked ready to pass out here today."

Sami had looked tired, purple smudges under her eyes. Jason wanted to pull her into his arms and tell her everything was going to be all right. He and Gabe would take care of her always.

He wasn't sure that would be welcome.

"I'm not sure she wants us to do right by her, Gran," he replied slowly. "I'm not sure she still wants us. And since when have you had termites?"

"Hogwash," Gran snorted. "She took one look at you two and you could see every emotion on her face. As for the termites, you can't be too careful. Since I was in here, it seemed like a good time to have the house tented."

Gabe threw back his head and laughed. "You knew Samantha would be coming here. You planned it, old woman. Admit it."

"Maybe I did plan it. She still loves you. I can tell."

Jason wanted to believe that with all his heart. He'd felt like a limb was missing when she had been gone. He'd become used to the pain but it never really went away.

Gabe pointed to his own chest. "It's me she's pissed at. I'm the one that has to make this better." He put his hand on Gran's lined one. "I will apologize, Gran. But she may not be able to forgive me. She might want Jason still, but she and I have some bad stuff between us. I don't know whether she can give me another chance."

Gran relaxed and smiled. "So you do still love her?"

Gabe chuckled. "I do. Or maybe I should say I still love the Sami I knew. She's probably changed, Gran. I know I have. If this is going to work, we're all going to have to fall in love. All over again. It won't be easy. There's a lot of water under the bridge."

"Are you willing to try?" Jason asked. "Are you willing to put in the work?"

Gabe nodded. "I am. There are no guarantees. She may not want a Dom who owns a BDSM club. You know how uptight Sami could be."

Jason remembered well. Sami had been self-conscious about her body and just about everything else. It had been hard for her to really let go during sex. She'd enjoyed it but always seemed to keep part of herself locked away.

Gran picked up her fork and began to eat her pot roast from the diner. "I appreciate how you've been honest about your club and all. Everyone thinks an old woman will be shocked. Hell, I've got stories that would curl your hair not the other way around." Gran pinned them both with a stare. "I hear you give pleasure lessons at the club to the men in town. Teach them how to make their women scream is how I heard it."

Jason felt his face go warm and Gabe's was the same. Gabe scraped a hand down his face. "Something like that."

Gran nodded. "That's good. You can use sex as a way to snare her. Make her fall in love with you physically. Where the body goes, the heart will follow is the old saying."

Jason's eyebrows went up. "They actually say that? Do you think that's fair to trap her with sex?"

Gran looked at him with exasperation. "Of course it's fair. You intend to make her happy, don't you?"

"Hell, yes."

"Then isn't it to her benefit? You're going to make her happy and take good care of her. That's not a punishment, boys. I want to see my granddaughter settled and happy before I die. Maybe even a grandchild or two." She shook her fork at them. "I got her to stay in your house. The rest is up to you. Don't waste any time. She's got that scared, 'I'm about to run' look. You need to make this happen."

Jason was back on his heels at her vehemence. "Got it. We'll do everything we can to make her fall in love with us again. For all of us to fall in love again."

Gabe rubbed his chin, a thoughtful expression on his face. "We only have one obstacle."

Jason blew out a breath. "Yep. We do have that."

Gran scowled. "What obstacle?"

Gabe sighed. "She doesn't trust me. She can't love me, really love me again, until she can trust me. Trust takes time."

Jason slumped against the wall. Time was something he didn't think they had much of. Sami could leave again at any moment.

Gran started eating her pot roast again. "I have an idea about that. Pull up a chair and I'll tell you all about it. This is for my granddaughter so we'll pull out all the stops."

* * * *

Samantha walked up the stairs of Jason's house, dragging her suitcase behind her. She'd basically brought almost everything she owned with the thought she might not be able to return to her apartment. She needed to give Sadie a call and see if anything had happened since this morning.

Samantha pushed open the door at the top of the stairs and knew immediately it was Jason's room. His scent was everywhere, and she dropped her suitcase on the floor and walked into the room even as her brain was telling her to turn around. She stopped in front of his closet, the door wide open and ran her hands over his uniforms, all hung up neatly and smiled at the clothes tossed carelessly on the bed. Jason had always been challenged when it came to cleaning up after himself.

She turned to leave but a framed photo on the bedside table caught her eye and she picked it up, tears welling in her eyes. The photo has been taken at one of the Plenty Christmas parties that seemed like a lifetime ago. All three of them had been happy and smiling, with her ensconced in the middle of Gabe and Jason, their arms slung across her shoulders. She looked young and happy without a care in the world.

It was a long time ago.

She carefully placed the picture back and headed out of the room and down the hall. The second door beckoned and she couldn't stop herself from peeking inside.

Gabe.

The room was spotless, everything in its place. Gabe liked things just so and had often been driven to his wit's end by Jason's haphazard housekeeping. She pulled back, unwilling to see if he, too, had a picture on his dresser. She headed to the door at the end of the hall. At the time she'd left, the entire upstairs had been demolished for renovation. The older homes in the historic district were beautiful but many needed a great deal of work and this home had been no exception. Jason and Gabe had lived in the downstairs, working on the kitchen and back porch and yard, saying they'd get to the upstairs eventually.

She pulled her battered suitcase into the room and gasped. The room was beautiful. What Jason had described as brown and blue was actually a warm chocolate brown paired with a light blue. The room was enormous and probably took up half the top floor. Against the wall flanked by two large windows was a gigantic four-poster bed. The furniture was two-toned with light and dark wood and she immediately knew that Gabe had made it with his own two hands. He'd always been a talented carpenter with a detailed eye. It must have taken him weeks to make the headboard alone.

She found two large closets and another oversized walk in closet before walking into a luxurious bathroom with a jetted tub, three sinks, and a huge shower. She walked out and sat down on the bed, overwhelmed by what she had seen.

They'd created this master suite for sharing. They intended to share it with the woman they loved. It was like a sword in her heart to realize she wasn't that woman. Hadn't been for some time. Everything in this room had been planned and built with their future in mind.

She was suddenly angry with them for putting her here. Putting her in a position to see this, something she'd never be a part of. She didn't belong here anymore.

She rummaged in her purse and pulled out the prepaid cell phone she'd purchased at the big box store a few days ago when her old cell had been destroyed. She punched in a few numbers and was relieved when Sadie answered on the second ring.

"Hey, girl. You make it to Plenty okay?"

"I did. Is everything okay there?" Sami held her breath.

"I haven't heard from him but I've been at work all day. Maybe he'll give us a few weeks of peace and quiet. Didn't you just pay him?"

She blew out her breath in relief. She hated to leave Sadie and

Trish, her other roommate, in the line of fire, but she didn't have a choice. She'd needed to come see Gran.

"I did. You remember what to tell him if he does come there or call?"

"Of course. I tell him you went to Atlanta to visit an old girlfriend. No mention of Plenty. When are you coming back? Or are you coming back?"

It had been Sadie who had given her the advice to take as much as she could fit in her suitcase. Sadie had even offered her money, but Sami wouldn't take it. Sadie didn't have much more than Sami did. In fact, all three of them, Trish included, were pretty much busted all the time. They all worked crappy menial, minimum wage jobs to keep a roof over their head and some food on the table.

"I don't know. Gran needs me right now. Maybe I can get some work while I'm here. I can't stay though."

"Why not? Seems to me the perfect place for you. You have people that care about you there, Sam. If I had family somewhere, I sure as hell wouldn't live like this."

Sami plucked at the bedspread. She'd only told Sadie a part of the story of why she's left Plenty. "It's complicated."

Sadie sighed. "There's a man involved then."

"It's not about a man." It was about *two* of them, actually.

"It's always about a man, honey. I've been there and worn the T-shirt. Don't let anyone chase you away from your family. Stay in Plenty. There's nothing to come back here for."

"Maybe. We'll see. Call me if you hear anything. Or I'll call you in a day or two. Miss you."

"Miss you, too. Don't worry about anything here, just worry about your grandmother."

Sami hung up the phone, shaking her head. She didn't remember the last time she wasn't worried. It was a part of her life now with no end in sight.

Chapter Two

Sami padded down the stairs, yawning and stretching. She'd had the best night sleep she'd had in a very long time. Gabe and Jason's home was located on a quiet street, much quieter than the apartment she shared with Sadie and Trish. The bed was luxurious in its comfort and she'd fallen asleep soon after arriving and slept straight through the night. The sun was already high in the sky. She'd slept almost fourteen hours in a row.

She came to an abrupt stop when she saw Jason in the kitchen pouring a cup of coffee. The delicious aroma practically lifted her up on her toes, pulling her into the room. Jason looked so handsome in his uniform that emphasized his wide shoulders and tight butt. The amazing thing was he had no idea how gorgeous he actually was. The man was oblivious. He turned and gave her a smile.

"Did you sleep okay? I looked in on you last night to see if you were hungry but you were dead to the world."

She wasn't sure how she felt about him seeing her while she slept. Maybe she'd started snoring in the last few years.

"I was pretty tired. I've been picking up as many shifts at work as I can."

"Coffee?" He grabbed another mug from the cabinet and she nodded, watching as he prepared her coffee exactly as she liked it.

He hadn't forgotten.

He handed her the mug and she sat at the table trying to think of something to say. After all this time, she didn't know what to say to Jason. He deserved more than an apology. She'd run out on him when he'd needed her the most. It didn't say much for her character.

Jason pulled a couple of pieces of toast from the toaster and plopped them on a plate and placing it in front of her.

"You missed dinner. You need this more than I do."

He grabbed the honey from the cabinet and sat it next to her plate.

Shit, he remembered everything.

She shook her head and pushed the plate toward him. "I can't eat your breakfast."

"Eat, and don't argue." Jason pointed to the plate and turned back to slide two more slices of bread into the toaster. She knew better than to argue with him and squeezed the honey on the bread before biting into it hungrily. She hadn't eaten since lunch and she was starved.

Jason settled with his own toast and coffee across from her. "What do you have planned today?"

She shrugged. "I'll go see Gran this morning. Maybe I'll call Lacey and Becca. I'd like to spend some time with them while I'm here."

"So you're not planning to stay?"

She sighed. Talking to Jason when he was in this mood had never been easy. "I'm here for Gran. Once she's better, I'll need to go back."

"To your job? It's nice of them to give you the time off to see Gran."

Her job wasn't nice at all. Her boss was a real prick and he'd fired her when she'd asked for the time off.

"Yeah, it's a great place to work." She couldn't believe she'd said that and hadn't been struck by lightning.

He stood up to pour himself more coffee. "Gran would like you to stay. She's not getting any younger, Sami. She needs you here."

Sami stared at her coffee cup. She felt like ten kinds of slime, but she wouldn't bring her problems into her grandmothers remaining years.

"I'll come visit more often." She played with her spoon. "Thank you for being here for her when I couldn't. I'm relieved you were there to find her when she fell."

Jason warmed up her coffee. "Actually, it was Gabe that found her. I was on duty and on the other side of town."

"I can tell you've both kept an eye on her. I'm thankful. Where is Gabe anyway?"

Jason nodded towards the stairs. "Still sleeping. He closed the club and probably didn't get to bed until four this morning."

"Club? What kind of club does he manage?"

Jason's mouth tipped up at the corners. "Owns. He owns a club at the edge of town. As for what kind of club, I'll let him tell you about it."

Things really had changed. She'd always assumed Gabe would become a carpenter and build furniture. She'd never pictured him as a businessman.

"Good for him. What else has changed?"

Jason stood up and rinsed out his cup, taking his time answering.

"Lots of things. Lots of people. New people have come to town, some have left. Like you. New businesses. Some things never change, of course." He grinned. "Tom and his wife still argue like cats and dogs. I swear Ryan's ready to pull his hair out."

That made Sami smile. Tom was a real character and his wife was something else entirely. No one in town blamed Tom for pissing off his wife so she wouldn't speak to him for a while.

"Do they still have bingo down at the firehouse?"

Jason chuckled. "They do. Charley's still closes early on that night."

Sami groaned and put her hand over her stomach. "I love Charley's pizza. It's the best pizza I've ever had."

"Then we'll go tonight. After we take dinner to Gran."

She swallowed hard. "I wasn't hinting around. I'm sure you have better things to do than entertain me while I'm here."

Jason leaned against the counter. "Is that your subtle way of asking if I'm seeing somebody, Samantha Jane?"

She hated being called by her full name and he knew it. He knew how she took her coffee and toast and he knew she was ticklish behind her knees and on her neck. He knew too damn much.

"It's none of my business if you're seeing someone."

She almost sounded convincing. Problem was, she wanted to know.

"I'm not. I've dated since you left, but I haven't been serious with anyone. I was hurt when you left."

There it was. He'd put it out on the table. His expression was bland as if he was discussing the weather or the new traffic light on Main and Oak.

She took a deep breath and gathered every ounce of courage she had. It was time to face the music. "I'm sorry I left the way I did. I thought I was doing the right thing at the time."

"Was it the right thing?"

She couldn't tell him how badly things had gone for her. Everything was a fucking mess.

"Hindsight can't change anything. I left and I've had to deal with the consequences of that decision."

"Gabe left not long after you did."

She nodded. "Lacey told me."

"I was alone. You both were gone. You both left me. For a time, I blamed myself."

Her gut burned with shame. Everyone had paid the price for her stupidity and selfishness.

"It wasn't your fault, Jason. I swear. You didn't do anything wrong."

"I know that now." He leaned forward, his palms flat on the table, looking her right in the eye. "I blamed Gabe for driving you away. That drove him away." He straightened up. "Then I blamed you."

"Do you still blame me, Jason?" She had to turn away from the intensity in his gaze. More than anything, she wanted to reach out and pull him close to her. She'd missed his body pressed tightly to her own. She'd missed being touched and loved by him. It was a constant pain in her heart she'd grown used to, and even encouraged. It had been her link to the past.

"Not any more. We all did the best we could at the time. None of us were equipped to handle the emotions and issues that Gabe and I came back with after Iraq."

Her eyes burned with tears. "Thank you for that. I still blame myself, though."

Jason grabbed his car keys. "Sounds like a waste of energy, sunshine. Forgive yourself." He headed toward the front door. "We'll eat out tonight. Have a good visit with Gran."

Her eyes welled with tears and she didn't try and stop their slide down her cheeks.

He'd called her *sunshine*.

* * * *

Lacey was grinning and waving when Sami walked into the new coffee shop in town. Josh's Java was near the Sheriff's office and Ryan Parks had spied her crossing the street and came out to give her a hug. He'd interrogated her about what she'd been doing since she left and why she'd stayed away so long. She imagined he was a very effective lawman if he questioned criminals the way he'd questioned her. She'd found herself stammering until he'd finally taken pity on her and invited her to dinner at his house so she could meet his new wife, Jillian.

Lacey jumped up from the table and pulled her into a bone crushing hug. "Girl, it's about time you came home. I've missed the hell out of you."

Sami rolled her eyes and settled herself at the table overlooking the street. It was a sunny and warm afternoon in Plenty and she felt herself relax as she absorbed the expressions of happiness on the faces of the residents. It had been a long time since she'd been around people who were truly happy and content with their lives.

"I've missed you, too. I heard you're living at home again. What's going on?"

A waitress appeared at their table and took their orders before Lacey could answer. Lacey was a miniature version of Jason with dark hair and twinkling blue eyes. Lacey and Jason had two other sisters who Sami adored, but it was Lacey she was the closest to. Lacey had the same sense of humor that never failed to crack them both up while others didn't even get the joke.

Lacey sighed. "I'm jobless. The economy's tough for recent graduates and since I want to stay here in Plenty it's even tougher. I have a degree in art and design. Shit, I should have been a nurse, but blood makes me nauseous."

"I remember. You almost passed out that time Jason cut open his leg playing tackle football in the backyard. Didn't he fall over a pottery planter?"

Lacey shuddered. "He did. I don't know how Mom did it. She just wrapped his leg up in a towel, tossed him in the back seat of the car, and took him to the doctor, cool as a cucumber."

"She was probably just as sick to her stomach as you were, but couldn't show it since she was the mom."

"I swear I'm never having kids. Poop, pee, blood, and puke. Why would anyone do that to themselves?"

Sami had often pictured herself having a baby with Gabe and Jason. "Babies are cute."

The waitress set their coffees down on the table. "Becca's little son, Noah, is a doll. Wait until you see him. He's going to have girls falling all over him when he gets older. Heck, he's got girls fawning on him now. He's super cute and works it."

Sami sipped her coffee. "Since you're out of work, I guess asking you how I might find a temporary job while I'm here is out of the question."

"What kind of work are you looking for?"

Sami shrugged. "Waitress, clean houses, run errands. I'm not picky. I just need to make some money." She leaned forward, not wanting this overheard. "I'm just about broke. There's always too much month at the end of my paychecks."

Lacey frowned. "I thought you got a great job at one of those fancy places for tourists?"

Sami plucked at her paper napkin. Lacey was a friend so it was okay to tell her, but she wasn't proud of the situation. She'd given Lacey the phone number to her new job, but never the details about it.

"I got laid off when a new corporation bought the hotel and brought in their own staff. Then I couldn't seem to find a new job that paid the same, so I took a job as a night desk clerk in another hotel. Then I had to quit that job due to some…difficulties. I took a waitress job, then I cleaned hotel rooms for awhile. My last job was as a waitress but, and please don't tell anyone, they fired me when I said I needed to come to Plenty."

Lacey's expression was sympathetic. "Shit, I'm sorry. I knew you weren't at the original place, but I didn't realize things were that bad. It sounds like it hasn't been easy."

"It hasn't. I wish I'd never left Plenty, but you can't turn back the clock."

"Oh honey, I'm so sorry."

Sami swallowed the lump that had formed in her throat. "I just hit a rough patch. Everything will be fine."

They chatted for a few minutes more than Lacey looked at her watch and scowled. "I have to go. I promised Mom I would pick her up from her dentist appointment. They gave her laughing gas and she hates to drive afterward."

Sami hugged Lacey. "Tell her hi from me. I miss her."

"She's going to insist you come over for dinner one night."

Sami had fond memories of Jason's mother. She'd never judged Sami for her somewhat less than stellar family tree. Both of Sami's parents were drunks and ne'er do wells. Gran had been the only real parent Sami had ever known.

"That would be good. If I can have breakfast with your brother, I can have dinner with your mom and dad."

Lacey shoved her phone into her purse. "I think my brother wants to have more than breakfast with you, but I promised you I wouldn't talk about that."

Sami shook her head. "It's too late. I wish it wasn't, but it is."

"I'm not so sure about that. Jason hasn't been serious in the least with anyone since you left. I think he still loves you. When we were decorating the house for Christmas, Mom found your Christmas stocking. Jason's expression bordered on tortured."

"I can't deal with this right now. I need to concentrate on Gran and making some money."

Lacey stood, gathering up her purse and keys. "I'll leave it for now, but not forever. I want you to stay and if I have to play dirty to do it, I will."

That made Sami laugh. This tiny, dark haired sprite acting tough was hilarious. "I'm terrified."

"You should be," Lacey called over her shoulder. "Call you tomorrow."

Lacey disappeared down the block and Sami finished the last of her coffee. A handsome man came over to clean the table.

"Welcome to Josh's Java. I'm Josh, the owner. You must be Samantha."

Sami groaned. "The gossip moves just as fast as it did a few years ago. Maybe faster."

"Well, we have Wi-Fi now." His smile was teasing and she liked his easy-going manner.

"I am Samantha, but everyone calls me Sami. It's nice to meet you."

"It's nice to meet you. Can I get you anything else?"

She shook her head. "Actually, I don't suppose you're looking for any help here are you? I'm looking to pick up some work while I'm in town. I'm an experienced waitress."

Josh rubbed his chin and then smiled. "Actually, I do know of something. Not here, but someplace else. I had someone in here today that was saying they're having trouble finding competent help."

Sami nodded eagerly. "I do have experience. I've been waiting tables for a little over a year."

Josh looked over his shoulder as another customer waved to him. "I'll write down the information and you can go talk to him. Are you open-minded?"

That was a weird question. "Um, yeah. I guess so."

"Good. Let me write down the address." Josh looked at his watch. "He's probably there now, getting set up for tonight. You might be able to catch him."

Sami was going to impress the hell out of this guy. She desperately needed this job.

"Thank you so much, Josh. I can't tell you how grateful I am."

"No problem. I'm glad to be able to help two people. It's a win for everyone."

Sami felt her burdens get a little lighter. If she could get a job, things would really be looking up.

* * * *

The address led to the building where Leah and Gabe's dad had an auto repair shop. All the old signage had been pulled down and replaced with one smaller, discreet sign on the side of the building in black with gold lettering—Original Sin. She tried the door next to the sign but it was locked and she was starting to turn away when the door swung open.

"I thought I heard someone out here. Come on in."

Gabe stood in the doorway, looking incredibly handsome in faded blue jeans and a white button-down shirt with the sleeves rolled up. His arms were tan and muscular, sprinkled with a smattering of golden hair. She resisted the urge to reach out and run her hand over his arms and up to his wide shoulders. She knew his skin would feel warm and his body firm under her fingers. She'd always loved the contrast between their hard, male bodies and her soft, feminine one.

"I think there's been a mistake."

She started to back toward her car, but he stepped forward and caught her hand in his, sending a streak of lightning through her so strong it almost brought her to her knees. It had always been like this with Gabe and Jason.

"Why don't you come in and tell me about it and maybe we can fix whatever mistake's been made?"

She didn't want to be alone with him but he tugged gently on her arm and she found herself following him inside. She could have pulled away at any time but her heart wanted to be near him more than she wanted to run away.

They entered a large room with high ceilings and warm furnishings. There were couches scattered around the room, along with several tables and chairs that looked suspiciously like something Gabe would have made himself. The focal point of the room was the large dark oak bar at the far end with a mirrored wall behind it.

"This is beautiful. You did the woodwork."

She didn't phrase it as a question and he didn't take it as one. He simply smiled and motioned toward an overstuffed couch.

"Relax. Can I get you a soda or something?"

She perched on the edge of the couch. "No, thank you. I just came from the coffee shop actually."

He sat on the couch and she had to steel herself not to reach for him. Touching him was a habit she couldn't indulge. He leaned back and stretched out his long legs.

"So tell me about this mistake."

She gripped her handbag on her lap. "Josh said he knew someone looking for a waitress. I didn't realize it was you."

The corner of Gabe's mouth tipped up. "I am looking for a

waitress. Are you applying? I need the help badly."

She shook her head. "I think it would be a very bad idea."

Gabe pursed his lips. "I don't know about that. It sounds like you need a job and I need a waitress. Seems like it would suit everyone."

She exhaled in frustration. "Don't be deliberately obtuse. I can't work here."

He sat up and leaned his elbows on his knees. "Because I was an asshole and things didn't work out? Are you worried about me losing my temper and control? I can assure you it won't happen. You may not believe me but I've changed these last few years."

"You do seem different." That was an understatement. The old Gabe wouldn't have been this calm and matter of fact. He'd been a wild man, racing his motorcycle on the back roads and being loud and boisterous. This Gabe was quiet and almost contemplative.

Gabe nodded. "I am, but I don't expect you to be able to trust that without seeing it. I understand I broke your trust. I hurt you. I'm sorry about that, Samantha. You'll never know how much."

Her heart ached in her chest. "You're the only one who calls me by my full name."

He smiled. "Jason does when he's teasing you."

"I didn't mean my whole name. I meant just Samantha."

"I know. I always wanted to have something that was just ours."

His voice was soft, almost caressing and she felt her entire body responding, waking up after a long winter's sleep.

"I'm sorry, too. I told Jason this morning and I'm saying it to you now. I'm sorry I ran out the way I did."

Gabe shook his head. "You don't owe me any explanations or apologies. I did some bad things."

"It didn't mean I should leave. I wish I'd stayed."

"It never would have worked out for us if we'd all stayed here." He reached out and brought her fingers to his lips sending wave of heat through her body. "We would have crashed and burned for sure. I needed to go away and figure out what I needed to do to get my life turned around. I guess you needed to go away too. My regret is that we left Jason here holding the bag so to speak. It wasn't fair to him, but shit, the way I was back then wasn't fair to any of us. I was out of control. Something had to change." He smiled a crooked smile. "So I changed my location."

"And it worked?"

He chuckled. "It was a start. When I left, I'd hit rock bottom with you. I knew I had to do something or I was going to die at an early age. I sought help from a psychiatrist. He sent me on the road to recovery."

"I'm glad. But I still don't think it's a good idea for me to work for you."

He gazed at her for a long time. "Got any better offers? You can make around three hundred a night here in tips. Five hundred on a weekend night."

Her eyes widened in amazement. That was way more than she made at the shit hole restaurant in Orlando.

"Wow, that's good money." She looked around. "You do that much business here? It doesn't look like it holds that many people."

He laughed, a warm, rich sound that sent a shiver up her spine. "This is a private, members only club which means each check has a minimum tip on it. They can also tip extra if they wish, and they often do. This is also just the front room. If you want to make three to five hundred a night, you have to work the back room as well. That's where the big money is."

She craned her neck, looking for another door. "There's another room?"

He pointed to a long set of drapes at one end of the room, off in the corner. "Behind those drapes is a door with a key card lock on it. The backroom is behind that door. Are you interested in taking a look?"

She nodded, overcoming her reticence. It was too much money to turn down. Money like that could make a real difference in her life.

"Sure, if you don't mind."

He stood up and pulled her to her feet. "I don't mind at all. Just one question. Do you still have an open mind?"

That was the second time someone had asked her that. "Are you running some sort of illegal gambling back there, Gabe? Is that what this is about? I won't be involved with something that's against the law."

She'd learned her lesson.

"No, sweetheart. Ryan would kick my ass if I did anything illegal. This isn't illegal, it's simply…unusual, I guess you would say. I don't think it's immoral, but it is unusual."

Her curiosity was piqued. "If it's not illegal, bring it on."

She marched over to the curtain and waited. He chuckled. "Just remember you wanted to see this. I didn't drag you back here."

He was making her crazy with his mysterious statements. This was the Gabe she remembered. He'd loved to tease her.

"Just show it to me already. What do you have back there, a torture chamber?"

He pulled the curtain aside and swiped a card through a reader, the door beeping, and popped open. He pushed it wider and allowed her to walk in first, flipping on lights. It was only when the last light when on she realized why he'd been so shady. She knew her mouth was hanging open in shock and tried to close it but each time she did she saw something even more shocking. She turned to him, aghast at what he'd revealed.

"Are you out of your fucking mind?"

Chapter Three

Samantha was taking it better than he'd expected. Her face was bright red and her mouth was gaped open like a fish, but she hadn't run from the room screaming so that was a positive sign.

"I haven't lost my mind, although I can see you're not convinced."

She shook her head and started to walk around, looking at the toys in the dungeon room closely. Her first stop was the St. Andrew's cross against the far wall. She ran her hands over the smooth surface and his mind crowded with vivid memories of those same fingers stroking his own skin. Dangerous thoughts.

She moved to the bondage table, her brow furrowed as she examined the clips on the corners of the table. She appeared to be trying to figure out how the table worked. He chuckled and decided to help her. He'd been worried how she would take this news, but this was better than he'd hoped for. She'd become defiant instead of sliding into some puritan shock.

"The cuffs hook to these carabineer type clips. The submissive lies on the table and his or her wrist cuffs are clipped here." He pointed to the top corners of the table. "And their legs are bent up, spread, and clipped to the bottom corners here. They're open and ready to be used for their Dominant's pleasure."

She continued her tour of the dungeon, and he watched her expression carefully. She didn't appear disgusted, more like intrigued. She wasn't the submissive type but it didn't mean they couldn't have some fun in here. Snorting, he realized he was getting ahead of himself. He wanted her but nothing about this relationship was a given. There were things that needed to be talked about first.

She had moved to the area with spanking benches and a pair of wooden stocks. Every now and then she'd turn to him, start to open her mouth to ask him something, snap it shut, and move on to look at something else. Finally, she stopped in front of a wall of floggers and whirled around, poking him in the chest.

"I suppose this is funny to you? Start talking and don't stop until you've told me everything."

There was no way he could tell her everything. What he'd seen in Iraq stayed in Iraq. He and Jason had agreed on that. They couldn't shelter her from everything, but the realities of war were something she didn't need to know about.

"What do you want to know?"

He knew what she wanted to know but he wanted to make her say it. She'd always been shy when it came to talking about sex or body parts. If they were going to fall in love with each other again, she would have to move out of her comfort zone. He didn't need to tie her up and beat on her. He'd become a Dominant as a way to learn to control his emotions after leaving the service. He did need her to understand that what consenting adults do was okay. People in the lifestyle didn't have a mental defect. They weren't crazy. They simply had different needs, not all of them sexual.

She gave him a look that said he was a fucking asshole and he had to hide his chuckle. They may not have been together for the last few years but they still knew how to push each other's buttons.

She waved her hand. "This is what you're into now? You're some sort of Marquis de Sade?"

"No." He leaned down and looked into her almost amethyst eyes. "No, I am not a sadist. I am a Dominant man. I opened this club a few months ago. It's been successful. It brings people into Plenty from all over central Florida. I'm a fucking pillar of the community, sweetheart."

Her eyes went wide. "You mean the town council knows what's

going on in this room? It's not a secret?"

He grinned. "No secrets. I let them know exactly what I wanted to do. Hell, there are enough alpha males in this town alone to keep me in business but I have friends in the lifestyle all over Florida and the word got around. Stan's fishing cabins are filled almost every night of the week plus a waiting list. It's brought in tourist dollars, my sweet. In fact, they're talking about building a hotel to make it easier. Right now, most of them have to stay in Tampa or Orlando."

She stepped back and almost fell over the spanking bench so he had to reach out and catch her. He set her on her feet but didn't let go of her soft satiny skin. He wouldn't mind seeing her cute little fanny draped over it as she was in desperate need of good spanking. Between both him and Jason, they'd spoiled the ever-loving hell out of her. That's why she'd run in the first place when things got tough. She'd always assumed he and Jason would take care of everything.

She pulled her arm away and perched on a padded portion of the bench, the wind clearly taken out of her sails.

"Plenty with a torture chamber. I didn't expect to come home to that."

She was yanking his chain to get a rise out of him, but he wasn't going to let her. He had better control and patience these days. She knew very well what BDSM was. He distinctly remembered a party over in Daytona they'd attended during bike week about five years ago. As the evening had worn on, the party had moved in a wild and raunchy direction. With his knowledge now, Gabe recognized it as very light amateur stuff, but it had certainly sparked some hot and heavy sex between the three of them back at their hotel.

He arched an eyebrow. "I don't remember you being this judgmental that weekend in Daytona."

She turned a deep shade of crimson, her eyes dropping to the floor. The submissive gesture sent fire through his veins and made his cock harden painfully in his jeans. "I don't know what you're talking about."

"You know exactly what I'm talking about. The people in the lifestyle are doing this consensually. The motto in the lifestyle is Safe, Sane, and Consensual. We adhere strictly to that here at the club. Anyone who violates it is no longer welcome here."

Her head came up, her expression challenging. "This is your lifestyle now?"

He shrugged. "It has been for the last few years. It helped me get control of my anger issues. It taught me a lot about myself. It saved me really." He crossed his arms over his chest. He didn't like her prissy tone. "Jason and I should have put you across our knees on occasion. You wouldn't have this attitude if we had."

Samantha jumped up. "You've got nerve. When did I ever deserve to be spanked?"

Gabe remembered a certain night well. Samantha and Lacey had gone to Ybor City, a party area of Tampa, where there was a bar every three feet. It was known for being wild, crazy, and sometimes dangerous. They'd stayed out all night partying, had breakfast at a local diner, then arrived back in Plenty smelling of beer and cigars around nine in the morning. He and Jason had waited up all night for her and by the time she'd shown up they'd been pretty ticked. She hadn't even bothered to call them to let them know she'd be gone all night.

"How about the night you and Lacey partied in Ybor while Jason and I paced the floor thinking you were dead in ditch somewhere?"

Samantha had the grace to look ashamed. "I apologized for that. Nothing happened," she protested, but he put his hand up. They didn't need to litigate this all over again. That wasn't the point anyway.

"You were fortunate that night. We wouldn't have been angry but we didn't even know where you were."

She nodded. "I should have called. I'm sorry you stayed up all night worrying about me. It was selfish on my part."

"You apologized then, although this apology looks much more sincere. If we'd spanked you we would have cleared the air then instead of still dealing with this now."

She was wringing her hands together. "It's just it wasn't fair, Gabe."

He knelt in front of her and took her hands in his, her clean scent surrounding him. "What wasn't fair, sweetheart? Talk to me."

"You both were older, and well, you were always telling me what to do. How could I grow up when you treated me like a child?" Her eyes grew dark with accusation. "But you did stupid stuff as well. I didn't get to lecture you. It wasn't fair."

Gabe exhaled slowly. He remembered it differently. "You punished us. You'd not talk to us for a few days. You'd flirt with other guys right in front of us. But, no, you didn't get to spank us."

He came to an instant decision. Fair was fair. He stood up and marched over to the wall where several items for impact play were hanging from hooks. He pulled down a medium impact crop.

He walked back to her and held it out. "You can punish me right now. I'll bend over this spanking bench and you can whip my ass for all the things I did."

He'd surprised her. Good. She needed something to shake her out of this malaise she was in.

"You have to be joking. You'd never in a million years let me use that on you. Not the macho man, Gabe Holt."

"Gabe Holt is a changed man, sweetheart. I'm completely serious. You want to even the score? Here's your chance."

It was a huge chance to let her whip him with the crop. He didn't know how much anger she had bottled up inside, but this was one way to find out. Maybe a really stupid way, but he'd never been all that bright when it came to her. It would get all the cards on the table, though, and that was a good thing. He needed to break through the brittle shell she'd built around herself. He could do it by strapping her to the spanking bench but she wasn't ready for that in the least. The only option was a reversal. She needed some sort of catharsis and he was in a position to give it to her.

She tentatively reached out and took the crop, her chin lifting with determination. "How do I use this thing?"

He took the crop from her and braced his leg on the bench before bringing it down on his calf smartly. She winced as it whistled through the air and jumped when it landed with a crack. It sounded much worse than it actually hurt since he had complete control of the implement and was wearing heavy jeans.

"It's all in the wrist and elbow. Don't swing from the shoulder, you'll wear yourself out quickly. Take your time. Aim carefully." He pointed to his kidneys. "Don't hit over the kidneys. Keep it in the soft area of the buttocks or the backs of the thighs."

She pressed her lips together nervously and nodded. He draped his body over the bench and gave her the thumbs up. "Go ahead, sweetheart. Time to make things fair and even."

At first he thought she was going to chicken out, but she took a deep breath and raised her arm, bringing the crop down on his ass weakly. It was barely a love-tap. She had more anger in her than that. He waited while she realized he wasn't going to hop up and say they were done. He needed her to get mad and let go of the emotions she held on to so tightly.

She brought down the crop again, this time a little harder but still not hard enough to do any real damage or even make him wince. He'd had much worse at the hands of a stony-faced Domme when he'd been in training to become a Dominant. You couldn't dish out a punishment until you'd learned what it was like to take one.

He'd definitely learned about fairness. And karma.

The third time had some vinegar behind it, the fourth, just about the same. By the time the fifth one landed, something had broken loose inside her and he saw tears spring to her eyes and roll down her cheeks. She started raining blows down on him, not aiming anywhere in particular and probably hurting her shoulder more than she was hurting him. Her anger made her movements sloppy and eventually she tossed the crop aside and crumpled to the floor in a sobbing heap.

He levered up from the bench and scooped her into his arms, carrying her over to a sofa tucked in a corner. There were places strategically around the playroom floor for aftercare and these next few minutes with Samantha were going to be the most challenging aftercare of his life. What was done and said could make or break any future they had together.

No pressure. She was simply the only woman he would ever love.

He patted her back and stroked her hair. "Let it all out, sweetheart. Cry and let go of all the bad stuff. That's a good girl. When you're ready, tell me what you're upset about. Tell me what you're mad about."

She cried and squirmed, kicking and punching at him for awhile longer, then finally lifted her face, all puffy and red. "I'm mad at you, Gabe. I'm mad and I'm hurt. Did you fuck her, Gabe? Was she hotter than me? Did you even fucking care about her?"

Finally, a breakthrough. She'd said the words. Now they could start to heal and move forward.

* * * *

Sami was exhausted in Gabe's arms, the pain in her heart so excruciating she wanted to crawl away and die. She'd stopped feeling things this deeply long ago and now she remembered why.

He pressed a kiss to her damp forehead and stroked her hair back from her face. "I didn't have sex with her, Samantha. I loved you. I got drunk and almost got into a fight. Another fight. She was working the bar that night and drove me home. She wanted to but I said no. Hell, I wasn't in any shape to do anything if I wanted to, which I didn't. It was late and we both fell asleep. You walked in and thought the worst. Rightly so. It took me awhile to sober up and realize I hadn't cheated on you. It didn't matter though because I'd done something much worse." He looked as haunted as she felt. "I'd disappointed you. I'd shamed you. I'm so sorry, baby. I am so very sorry for my behavior when I came back from Iraq. I wish I could go back in time and change it, but I can't. I can only say I'm sorry and that I never, ever betrayed you. You were my world, Samantha. You were what kept me sane when I came back."

She shook her head. "I didn't do a very good job then. You were crazy when you came back. Uncontrollable." There'd been so many bar fights. So many times Gabe had been drunk and angry. "You were angry all the time and I never understood why. Jason wasn't that angry."

He nodded, his expression sad. "I processed what I'd been through differently than Jason. We're not the same person, you know."

"I know that," she protested, but deep in her heart she knew she was guilty of treating them the same instead of as unique individuals.

"Really? How come I got a fishing pole on my last birthday that we spent together? I don't like to fish. Jason does."

She chewed on her lower lip. "I guess, maybe, I did stuff like that. I guess I wasn't a very good girlfriend."

His arms tightened around her. "Don't say shit like that. We loved you. You were an awesome girlfriend. Do you think we gave a shit about stuff like that? We didn't. It just meant we had to work harder for you to see us as separate individuals."

She laid her head on his shoulder as his words sunk in to her brain. "You really didn't have sex with her?"

"I really didn't. You're the only woman I've ever been in love with. I would never screw around on you."

She didn't want to think about what he'd been doing the last two years. She'd dated herself, although that had been a disaster, and Gabe was a devastatingly sexy man. She was sure there had been women. She didn't have to dwell on it though.

"I'm sorry I left. I should have stayed. You know, the better or worse stuff."

She heard his chuckled and felt the rumble in his chest. "We weren't married yet, and I think I brought the 'for worse' part to new lows. I couldn't expect you to stick around and deal with my self-destructive behavior."

Sami clung to him, loving how strong he felt. She needed his strength so badly right now.

"Are you okay now? You seem, well, better."

He tipped her chin up so she could look into his eyes. "I am better. It took time and therapy. I started seeing a professional to help me. He's the one that got me into the BDSM scene. I learned to control my emotions there. I rarely drink now, just a beer now and again. If I'm angry about something, I just say that I'm angry and find healthy ways to channel it like working out."

She ran her hands up his arms to his muscular shoulders. "You are looking pretty buff. You were hot before, but now…"

He angled her so she was practically lying on her back. "Thank you. You don't look too bad yourself, although you could do with a little more meat on your bones. What are you doing, starving yourself?"

He had no idea how hard she'd had to work just to pay the rent and keep the lights on. There hadn't been much money and she'd depended on her waitress jobs to provide her with a hot meal each day.

She elbowed him in the ribs. "It's fashionable to be slim. I was too fat before."

He got nose to nose with her. "If you were my submissive, I'd spank you for that. You were not fat. You had curves. Curves I liked pressed against my body."

She remembered well. Gabe would have kept her naked if she'd allowed it. She'd been too modest at the time, but for some reason the idea appealed to her now. They'd talked honestly. Maybe for the first time ever, and it made her feel freer than she'd felt in a long time.

"I'm not your submissive." She pushed herself up and looked around the room. It looked like a dungeon on steroids but she could see Gabe's touches everywhere. It looked like he'd built many of the pieces in here. She wasn't sure she was very submissive but she was sure she needed the cash. She was okay with adults doing whatever they wanted while she served them drinks.

"How about a tour of this joint? You can explain all of the equipment to me and explain this whole Dominant submissive stuff."

He blinked in surprise. "You want me to give you a tour? A real tour?"

She untangled herself from his arms and stood up. "Yep, if I'm going to work here, I need to understand everything that's going on, don't you think?"

His smile was blinding. "I do think so. Let's start over here." He pointed to the large wooden *X*. "That's a St. Andrew's cross."

She followed him around as he explained each piece of equipment. She felt happier and lighter than she had in a long time. It felt good to apologize and it felt even better to know Gabe had never cheated on her. His apology had been sincere and his new demeanor chipped away at the fortress she'd built around her heart.

She wasn't sure she could keep her heart safe from these men much longer. They'd become more than she'd ever imagined, and in such stark contrast to who she'd been around since she'd left Plenty. She hadn't realized what fine men they were until she'd met men who redefined the word *scumbag*.

She was in serious danger of falling in love with them all over again.

Chapter Four

Sami bit into one of Charlie's breadsticks and hummed in appreciation.

"Damn, I've missed these. They just melt in your mouth."

Jason grinned. "They are good. Save room for the pizza, sunshine. You don't want to miss that."

She didn't want to miss the pizza. It felt like she hadn't eaten in weeks, her stomach growling as she devoured the bread. Gabe passed her another one.

"Samantha's going to come work for me at the club, Jason. Pick up a few shifts, help me out, make some extra cash."

Jason cleared his throat. "So does she know the club's...theme?"

Sami rolled her eyes. "I'm a grown woman, Jason. Did you think I'd faint dead away in shock?"

Gabe sat back in the booth with a smile. "I thought you'd run screaming from the room calling me a pervert. You surprised me, sweetheart."

Her heart pounded faster as he stretched his arm out and laid it on her shoulders. She could feel the warmth from his body next to hers. They'd both managed to break down her defenses in less than twenty-four hours. She didn't have the luxury of wanting them, but she couldn't seem to stop herself.

"Good. I hope I'm not the naive girl who left Plenty. I've seen some of life and I'm not that easily shocked."

Most of what she'd seen hadn't been good. A BDSM club seemed pretty minor when she put it all in perspective.

Jason studied her face. "You do seem less naive." He pointed to the doorway with a wink. "I forgot to tell you. Gabe and I planned a surprise for you. A few people are joining us for dinner."

She'd wondered why they'd insisted on a giant booth in the corner. They'd sandwiched her in on one side, leaving the entire opposite side free. She looked over past Jason and almost jumped out of her seat. Becca Parks was walking toward them with a big smile, two gorgeous men, and a baby, being held by the dark haired man. Jason chuckled and slid out of the booth so she could launch herself at her long-time friend.

"Oh, my gosh, I didn't know you were coming tonight. Are these your husbands? Is this little Noah? He's so cute! You look amazing!"

She was babbling but she didn't care. Tears sprung to her eyes and she hugged Becca again. She'd missed her friends and she'd missed this town. Sadie and Trish were good friends, but she and Becca had known each other since childhood.

The men settled the baby, who looked about nine months old, into a high chair at the end of the table and then all three of them sat down. Charlie had drinks and more garlic bread sticks in front of them in a flash.

Becca pointed to the dark haired man opening a small container of cheerios. "This is Travis, my husband." Then she pointed to the blond man on her right. "And this is my other husband, Mark, and this little guy who is about to make a mess with his dinner is our son, Noah."

Introductions were made and Becca, who had never been shy, wagged her finger. "Tell me you're staying. Say it now. I'll even let you babysit Noah."

"I'd love to babysit Noah. He'd the cutest baby ever. I'm here until Gran gets better. After that, well, I have a life in Orlando."

Not much of one. A really crappy one, to be honest. She wanted nothing more than to stay, but she didn't want to bring her problem with her.

Becca narrowed her eyes and gave her a suspicious look. She always had been perceptive and Sami squirmed in her seat trying to look sincere about wanting to leave Plenty.

"You don't want to leave. You want to stay here. You should stay here. You could open the B and B back up. We need a hotel here in Plenty now that Diamond Jim has opened his club and Justin Reynolds opened his. They bring in out of towners like crazy."

She turned to Gabe. "She called you Diamond Jim. Are you rich? Since when did you get rich?"

Gabe had always done okay making furniture, but he'd never been what you would call wealthy. He'd usually spent any extra money on his Harley or his truck.

Gabe shrugged, obviously uncomfortable. "I wouldn't say I'm rich. I made some good investments the last few years. Starting a new business can be expensive. I've been lucky the community has embraced Original Sin."

Mark laughed. "Nothing this town loves more than sin. You're being too modest. That parking lot is filled to the brim every night you're open. Are you thinking of opening up seven nights a week?"

"No way," Gabe shook his head. "Five nights a week is enough. God only needed one day of rest, but I'm a mere human. I need at least two." He turned to Sami. "Becca's right. You should open the B and B back up. It's a sure thing."

She would love to do that very thing. "It was run-down when I left. You said it's being tented for termites. It would need too much work," she protested.

"We'll help," Jason pointed to himself and Gabe. "The structure is sound. Some paint, refinish the floors, upgrade the furniture and you're in business."

"It sounds expensive." Sami had about fifty bucks in her purse.

Gabe pursed his lips in thought. "I'd be willing to invest in it. After all, I'd be getting a chunk of the benefit from it."

"Do you have the money to invest?" she gaped.

"I don't think it will be as expensive as you're imagining." Jason put his hand over Sami's. "I can help out with money if need be. It would be a good thing for you and a good thing for Plenty. We could talk to Zach and Chase about doing any of the real heavy work."

Becca laughed. "Sounds like it's a plan. I love it!"

Even baby Noah was clapping his hands together and grinning, two pearly white teeth just breaking through his gums. Sami didn't know what to say. She wanted to stay more than anything. She wanted to find a way to be with these two amazing men, find forgiveness for all of them. Could she really hide from the ugliness in Orlando?

"It's something to think about," she replied softly. She'd majored in business in college. Running the B and B would be right up her alley.

Travis wiped off Noah's hands and face with a napkin. "I realize I'm a newcomer here, but as a member of the town council, I'd like to urge you to think about doing this. We've spent the last several meetings talking about a lack of lodging in Plenty for the people who visit. We're losing revenue to Tampa and Orlando, and the tourists aren't happy about having to make the long drive back and forth. If money is an issue, we could probably arrange a small business loan for you."

Five pairs of eyes were focused on her expectantly. They'd swept away all her objections and paved the way to making it even easier than she'd ever imagined. Her heart wanted to stay in Plenty. She'd never wanted to bring trouble there, but perhaps she could keep a low profile. He might give up and leave her alone now that she was gone.

"I'd like to," she said slowly, looking at Gabe and Jason. "If you'll help me."

Both men grinned and high-fived above her head. "Excellent," Jason crowed. "We can start tomorrow getting things cleaned up and making plans. I have the day off."

Gabe nodded. "I'll help, too. We'll make sure the club gets closed promptly at two and head home to get some sleep so we'll have the energy to tackle this."

Becca arched an eyebrow. "We? Are you working at the club, Sami?"

Sami lifted her chin. "I am. I'm helping Gabe out while I'm here."

Becca leaned across the table. "We've been a few times. It's hot, if you know what I mean. Your boyfriend knows his way around a flogger."

Becca's voice was low but not so low the whole table couldn't hear her. Sami felt herself flush when Gabe was referred to as her boyfriend. She peeked up from under her lashes and he had a smile on his face. "I like the sound of that, Becca. Samantha's boyfriend. Hmmmm…it has a ring to it."

Sami dragged her gaze away from Gabe and back to Becca. "You've been to the club? You're a mother."

Becca giggled. "I'm a mother, I'm not dead from the neck down. We took Gabe's Bondage for Beginners class. It was fun. Everyone was having a good time and it's not like my boys had never tied me up before."

Sami slapped her hand over her face. "That's a visual I could do without." She turned to Gabe. "And you? Bondage for Beginners? I'm afraid to ask what else you teach there." He started to answer, but she held up her hand and shook her head. "No, I'll just be surprised. I'm getting used to all these surprises."

Mark chuckled and wrapped his arm around Becca. He looked at her with such love, Sami almost melted. She wanted to be loved and cherished that way. "I think what my beautiful wife was trying to express is that there's nothing wrong with a little spice in the bedroom, married or not."

Jason raised his glass. "Here, here. I'm all for spice."

Sami smiled and raised her glass. She could surprise people, too. "I agree. Here's to spice."

Sami sipped her ice tea and took in the friendly vibes all around her. She might be making a huge mistake trying to get the B and B open again, wanting to stay in Plenty. There was a small voice inside of her telling her she'd never be free of Ray. He'd find her and he'd make life miserable. There was a much bigger part that believed in the love she'd found in Plenty again. Somehow she'd lost her way and believed him when he'd said no one would protect her or love her.

She was loved by the people in this town. Lord knew she loved them. They would take her side and protect her, she was sure. If she was really lucky, she could start her life all over again.

* * * *

Sami's stomach was full and her heart happy when the three of them returned to the house after Charlie's. She still wasn't sure staying in Plenty was truly feasible, but after being with her friends, and with Jason and Gabe, she wanted it more than she could imagine.

"Go upstairs and put some jeans on. The night's not over yet." Gabe waved her towards the stairs. Both men had a shit-eating grin on their face and she knew from experience they had something up their sleeves.

"Why would I do that?" She'd learned not to give in too easily, otherwise the men would think they could get away with anything and everything.

Jason sighed. "Can't you do anything without an argument? You'll like it. Trust us."

She didn't really want to watch television or read a book. If they wanted her to put on jeans it could only mean one thing. They would be outside and the night was too beautiful to ignore.

"Fine. Give me five minutes."

She flew up the stairs, changed clothes, and was down with two minutes to spare. Gabe grinned in approval and handed her a heavy leather jacket.

"We're going for a ride."

Her heart leaped with excitement. She'd loved being on the back of Gabe's motorcycle. Gabe had already been dressed in jeans and had a leather jacket on as well. He pulled a helmet out of the foyer closet.

"What about Jason?"

Jason smiled and shrugged into a leather jacket. "What about me? Think I'm going to stay home and watch reality television? I'm going with you."

Sami frowned. How were all three of them going to ride Gabe's motorcycle?

"She's confused." Gabe laughed. "Let's get her outside so she can see what we're talking about."

She followed them out the back door and saw while she was changing they'd pulled not one, but two motorcycles from the garage at the back of the house.

"You have one, too?"

Jason nodded. "Yep. Got mine when Gabe came back in the spring. Isn't she a beauty?"

"She is, not that I know a thing about cycles." She turned to Gabe. "Is yours new? It doesn't look the same."

Gabe nodded and placed a helmet over her head. "It isn't the same. I bought a new one after an accident wiped out the old. Are you ready to ride? You can split time with each of us."

Gabe helped her on to the back of his motorcycle before mounting up and starting the engine. It rumbled to life between her legs, the power only increasing her awareness of both these men. They took off and headed straight for the roads out by the quarries.

It was a mild evening and the wind whipped at the hair that hung below the helmet. The sound of the engine, the vibrations underneath her, and the motion as they took each curve lulled her into a sense of peace. She leaned against Gabe, her arms wrapped around his waist. At one point, he took a hand and reached back and patted her thigh as if to soothe her but she was already relaxed and exhilarated at the same time. It was like flying and she closed her eyes and let the sensations wash over her until the bike finally slowed down and then stopped.

She opened her eyes and found the men had driven her to the clearing where they'd first proclaimed their love. Her heart squeezed in her chest as the memory of the night swamped her. She'd been so young and so in love, and it seemed so very long ago. She mourned her innocence but there was no going back. She was a new person now and people would have to get used to that fact.

She lifted the helmet off her head, hooking it on the back of the bike. Jason was pulling a big blanket from a saddlebag and shaking it out before laying it down for them to sit on. They settled on the blanket without saying anything, simply listening to the crickets and the rustle of the trees.

Gabe pointed into the sky. "Look. This is why we brought you here."

She looked up and the sight almost took her breath away. It was a full moon, big and bright in the night sky. With the helmet she hadn't been able to see it, but here in this clearing the moonlight shone down on them like sunshine at midday.

"It's a harvest moon," Jason said.

"It looks orange." Sami couldn't take her eyes off of it. She couldn't remember the last time she'd stood still long enough to notice the moon.

"It does," Jason agreed. "The harvest moon often has an orange cast. It's the full moon closest to the Autumnal Equinox."

"It's beautiful."

Gabe swept her hair back with his hand, stopping to caress her cheek. "You're beautiful. I've thought about you every day that we were apart. I know you only arrived in Plenty, but we're laying our cards on the table. We want you, Samantha. We know we can't go back, but we can go forward."

"It's so complicated." Sami's voice broke. She didn't want to mar the moment by talking about her ugly past. She wanted to savor this time, snug between the two men she could never forget. They'd haunted her but now they were real. She soaked in their warmth and strength, content to just be with them in this place.

"We first told you that we loved you here." Jason placed his hand over hers, stroking her fingers.

She shook her head and smiled. "That's not how I remember it. This was where I told you I was in love with you. I did it first. You did say it, but don't try and tell me you'd planned to say it because I wouldn't believe it. You looked shocked when I said it."

Jason picked up her hand and kissed her knuckles sending heat to every corner of her body. "We would have said it long before then but, dammit, you were so young. We didn't want to push you into something you weren't ready for. We wanted you to make the choice to be with us. When you said that you loved us it was the best day of our lives. Of course, we said it back. I know we didn't say it first, but it wasn't because we felt any less for you."

"You were always trying to take care of me."

Gabe held her other hand, his strength and warmth filling her heart. "Probably too much. We didn't let you stand on your own two feet and let you grow up. We coddled and spoiled you. We won't make that mistake this time."

"I'm certainly not spoiled now." If they only knew how she'd been living these last few years, they'd see she was a long way from spoiled.

"Maybe we'll spoil you a little." Jason chuckled. "But we know you need to be independent. We won't smother you."

"You never smothered me. Let's face it, I didn't always act very mature. I guess I wasn't ready to grow up."

"Because you didn't need to." Gabe shook his head. "We made that unnecessary."

She let the silence enfold them, not sure how to say what she needed to say.

"I'm not sure I can stay in Plenty. I know I said I would reopen the B and B, but there's so much you don't know. It might be a bad idea to move back."

Gabe tilted her chin up so she had to look them in the eye. They didn't look angry, only sad. Gabe pressed a soft kiss to her lips, leaving tingles when he lifted his head. "You're not leaving again. I can see you're scared of something. That's easy to see, sweetheart. But running isn't the answer any more. It's time to face your demons. Trust me, it will be worth it."

"I'm scared," she whispered.

"Give us a chance, sunshine." Jason's voice was soft and cajoling. "Give yourself a break. Every decision doesn't have to be made at this very moment. All we ask is you open your heart to the possibility of us. We want a second chance, Sami. Can you take a chance with us?"

Wanting them was stronger than her fear. With them she felt safe, after all. They were a haven in the storm her life had become. She couldn't deny them, or herself, this one thing.

"I will. You may be sorry I did, but I will."

Gabe kissed her again, slowly and thoroughly. She gripped his shoulders like a lifeline and let the goodness of being with them seep into her bones. When he was done, Jason kissed her. His lips were soft, but his kiss was hot, with a leashed passion and a hunger she could recognize. Both kisses were a promise of a future she desperately wanted to believe in.

Jason lifted his head, his expression unbearably tender. "We'd only be sorry if you left again. You complete this triangle, sunshine. We need you, and you need us."

That's what it all came down to in reality. She needed them. Even if she'd found success in Orlando, it wouldn't have mattered. Her heart had a hole only they could fill.

She'd been fooling herself to think she could leave Plenty now that she was actually here. Plenty was home and so were Jason and Gabe.

Chapter Five

"It needs a lot of work," Sami sighed. "A bunch."

Jason looked around the living room of the large Victorian home that had housed Plenty's one and only bed-and-breakfast for almost a hundred years. It needed some love but the bones of the house were in great shape.

"It won't be that bad. Paint, floors, some new furniture and it will look almost new."

Gabe strode in from where he was checking out the kitchen. "Put new appliances on the list. They work but they look at least twenty years old. If you're going to have guests here, you really need to have a modern kitchen."

"If they work, we shouldn't replace them," she protested. Dollar signs were whirring in her head as she calculated the cost for renovations.

Gabe had already moved on and was now checking the new floorboards that had been installed a few years ago just before she left. "They did a great job replacing the wood in here that was damaged by the busted pipe." He looked up at Sami. "You do need new appliances. New ones will be more energy efficient and will save on the power bill. In fact, I'm going to head to the garage and see how old the air conditioning in the house is. It might be better to replace it."

Gabe headed out to the garage and Sami turned to Jason. "Does he do that a lot now? Be bossy and take over? He didn't used to do that."

Jason laughed and grabbed her hand to head up the stairs. "He does. That Dominant training taught him confidence in making decisions and taking control. Personally, I'm happy. I don't have to be the one in charge all the damn time anymore."

Sami remembered well that Jason was always the level-headed one who made the major decisions. She and Gabe had been happy to follow along, although looking back Gabe had made his preferences known if he felt strongly about something. It's too bad she hadn't had them making decisions for her these last few years. Things might have gone much better for her. It certainly looked like their lives were better than ever, and hers was a big hot mess.

"Did Gabe follow in the Army?" She hadn't been able to talk to Gabe much about his experiences in Iraq. He'd been too angry, but she assumed he'd talked to Jason.

Jason chuckled. "Sunshine, Gabe was never a follower. Although there is a clear chain of command. I wasn't with him day to day, but he always had this inside of him. The confidence you see now was simply brought out of him, not created."

They walked in to the first of four bedrooms on the second floor. "You have a lot of confidence. I think you were born to be a lawman. Always calm and in control."

Jason checked the windows. "You make me sound boring as hell. I hope I have more to my personality than that."

"That's not boring. It's a good thing."

He crossed his arms across his wide chest with a wicked grin. "Women like bad boys. Like Gabe. Maybe I should get some leathers like he wears at the club."

She wrapped her hands around his wrist, his skin warm to the touch. "I like you just the way you are. You would look hot in leather pants, though." She closed her eyes. "I can see it now. Very hot."

His lips touched hers, the heat searing her soul and sending her arousal twisting in her belly. No matter how she tried to deny it, run from it, or plain ignore it, Jason was her man. If he wanted her, she was his. It was that simple and complex.

He pulled her closer, his hard body pressed close to hers, his tongue demanding entry past her lips. He took his time, as if this was the first time he'd ever kissed her, exploring her mouth and making her ache.

By the time he lifted his head, her body was ready for him. Her nipples were rock hard against the cotton of her bra, her panties drenched. His fingers were tangled in her hair and he gently extricated himself with a smile of regret.

"This isn't the time or the place."

She licked her lips, wanting to savor his taste. "You're right."

He lifted her chin so she was looking into his blue eyes. "It has to be both of us, sunshine. Are you ready for that?"

She swallowed hard. It was easy with Jason. They didn't have the angst between them she had with Gabe. Yes, she and Gabe had made strides in their relationship and things were much better. He seemed to be a changed man. She just needed to see she could trust it, that he wouldn't suddenly change back and become angry again.

"I'm not sure. I want to believe in Gabe's transformation."

Jason nodded. "I understand. I wasn't too sure about it when he came back to town, but I've seen it. It's real. You'll see it, too. Take the time you need."

"There are some things I haven't told you." The words almost stuck in her throat.

"If it's about guys while we were apart it isn't important. I don't care what you've been doing. That's the past. We need to think about the future."

He was making this too easy for her. "Do you not want me to know what you've been doing?"

"I haven't been a saint," Jason replied. "Neither has Gabe. We were all free agents and we've had other people in our lives while we were apart. No one, and I repeat, no one meant anything to me. You were, and are, it for me. You're the one woman I can't get over."

She licked her suddenly dry lips. This called for courage beyond anything she'd known before. "I couldn't seem to get over both of you. I wanted to. I tried to. But like most things since I left Plenty, it was a complete failure."

Jason frowned. "It sounds like you've had a hard time of it."

"That's an understatement. I need to tell you the truth before we can move forward."

Jason straightened up, his gaze appraising. "You never intended to do that, did you? You thought you'd come to town, sleep on Lacey's couch, avoid me and Gabe, and sneak back to Orlando when Gran got better? That was the plan wasn't it?"

She shook her head slowly. "Yes. I thought it would be better that way."

"Better for whom?"

Sami turned in surprise at Gabe's voice. "How long have you been standing there?"

"Long enough." His long strides ate up the distance between them. "In the spirit of full disclosure, I never got over you either, Samantha. You've haunted every day of my life since I left Plenty."

Tears started to well in her eyes. She'd been a fool to think she could come to Plenty and stay away from these men. It was sheer lunacy to think she could keep anything from them. She wanted to break down and tell them everything so she could feel their strong arms around her.

She sighed. "It can't be this easy."

Gabe chuckled. "Why make it complicated? We love each other, that's clear. Yeah, we've got stuff to work out, but isn't it better to work it out together instead of apart?"

She hated it when Gabe made sense. She couldn't argue against what he'd said.

"It still can't be this easy," she persisted. "We need to talk. More."

Jason shrugged. "She was always like this. She always liked to talk a subject to death."

Gabe nodded. "Okay, how about we finish putting the list together of what we need for the house, then we'll go back to the diner and we can talk. What do you want to talk about?"

She didn't really want to talk about anything, but she knew they needed to. "I guess we should start talking about what we've been doing since we broke up. You're the one who has changed so much. I need to believe in that change, Gabe. Maybe if you tell me about it, I'll have more confidence."

"Fair enough. It's not a very exciting story though. We'll talk and then we'll head to the club. Tonight's your first night of work. Are you nervous?"

She was, but she'd never admit it. "Of course not. I've been a waitress before. The work doesn't seem complicated."

Gabe grinned. "Glad to hear it. Let's get this work done. Sounds like we have a busy day ahead of us."

They continued touring the second floor, making notes when something caught their eye. Samantha tried to keep her mind on the task at hand, but her thoughts kept drifting. She was going to hear about their lives, but most importantly, she was going to tell them about hers.

She could only hope they'd still want her once they knew the truth.

* * * *

It was completely different than she'd thought it would be. The people at the club weren't strange, but friendly and quite normal once you got past some of the outfits and customs. Sami had quickly learned she needed to talk to the Dom or Domme and not the sub. Most subs weren't allowed to speak without permission and a few were even being led around by leashes.

At first, she'd been dismayed to see such treatment, but Gabe had pulled her aside and told her everything she would see was completely consensual. He'd even arranged for her to talk to a couple of submissives who assured her he was correct. They spoke of being cherished and loved by their Dominants and once Sami really looked she could see it was true.

She'd seen a Dominant feeding a sub by hand and even tenderly brushing her hair. It was in stark contrast to earlier when she'd seen the same Dominant spanking the sub with a paddle. She hated to admit it, but watching had turned her on. She'd had an erotic visual of Gabe and Jason paddling her bottom for some imagined infraction.

She recognized a few people but most of the clientele tonight were from out of town, according to Gabe. When she counted the number of people she was amazed. She really needed to get the B and B up and running.

She smiled at the bartender, Gary, letting him finish up with another patron. He'd been taking good care of her tonight, helping her learn patron's names and preferences. The hardest part of her job was keeping the member cards straight. All members who visited the backroom needed a special member key card that would unlock the door and record their entrance to the room. No member who visited the back room was allowed to have more than two drinks a night. The member would hand over their card when they ordered and she would give it to Gary to swipe through the computer when he filled the order. The computer would warn Gary when a member had reached their limit. As long as Sami didn't mix up the cards, everything was good. If anyone tried to exceed the limit, she was to notify Gabe, and not try and handle it herself.

She handed Gary the first card. "Gin and tonic and a Coke, light ice."

Gary pressed a few buttons and swiped the card with a grin. "Got it. Next?"

She handed him the second card. "Two ice waters. One with lime." He swiped the second card and handed it back.

"I'm on it. You're doing a good job tonight. You picked up the card system quick. Any more?"

"One more." She handed him the last card. "One Heineken and

one orange juice."

Gary pressed a few more buttons, swiped the card, and the machine buzzed. "Steve Samuels. He's already at his limit." He shook his head ruefully and pressed a button that would text Gabe's cell. "Steve's a rebel. He likes to drink before he even gets here. Gabe's had to escort him to the door twice already. He'll probably pull his membership this time."

Sami tensed. The last time she'd seen Gabe in a potentially volatile situation he'd ended up in a fight and had broken his hand and bloodied another man's nose. She didn't want to see a repeat of that tonight. Gabe came up behind her, his breath warm on her neck and his hand on her shoulder.

"I got a text. What's up?"

Gabe looked sexy as sin in black leather pants and vest, with heavy black boots. In the last few years, he'd gotten ink and now a tribal band tattoo circled his left bicep. When she'd seen him her body had flushed all over and her cunt had started dripping honey down her thighs. He looked like every bad boy fantasy she'd had come to life.

"Samuels. He's trying to order a third drink tonight." Gary handed Gabe the card and Gabe nodded grimly.

"I'm on it. Sami, I'll deal with this. You continue what you were doing. You're doing a great job tonight."

He flashed her a smile and headed for the backroom. She waited while Gary prepared her drinks and then headed to the backroom with her tray. She delivered the drinks and then moved to a spot where Gabe couldn't see her as he talked to Steve Samuels but she could see and hear him.

"As I said before, this is the third time. I have no choice but to revoke your membership."

Steve Samuels already looked angry but that statement seemed to enrage him. He bumped chests with Gabe in a piss-poor effort to intimidate him. Gabe didn't even bat an eye.

"Your rules are bullshit. I'm not even drunk. I can handle my liquor."

Gabe's expression was bland. "I'm sure you can. These rules are in place for the safety of all our members. No one who may have impaired judgment is allowed to scene. You have endeavored to circumvent our rules three times." Gabe held up the membership card. "Your tab is on me tonight. Would you like assistance to your vehicle?"

"Fuck you, Holt. You think you're a badass Dom, but you ain't shit."

Sami braced herself for Gabe's explosion. He would never let anyone talk to him like that. Samuels was about to get a broken jaw.

To her shock, Gabe's lips quirked and his arms crossed over his chest. "I'll take that under advisement. Now I'd like you to leave."

Samuels' sub was tugging on his arm, urging him to leave. Sami's knees almost gave way in shock when his arm reared back and he backhanded the pretty sub. She stumbled over the bench and fell to her knees on the floor.

"That was a mistake." Gabe nodded to one of the monitors that he had work the back room. "Call Sheriff Ryan."

Apparently, Samuels decided he had nothing to lose and he took a swing at Gabe. In Samuels's inebriated state, Gabe easily ducked and grabbed the man's arm, wrenching it so it was behind his back so he was incapacitated. Gabe reached onto his belt and unclipped a set of handcuffs, quickly cuffing his wrists together.

Sami knelt down and checked to see if the woman was okay, helping her to her feet. A cursory once over showed the woman was going to have a black eye tomorrow but nothing seemed to be broken.

Sami winced in sympathy as the woman held her hand to the side of her face. Sami dug the bar towel out of her waistband and dumped the ice cubes from an empty glass into towel, placing it on the woman's eye.

Gabe gave her a look of appreciation and beckoned the monitor who had called Ryan. "Watch him until the Sheriff gets here." He turned to the sub, pulling the ice pack away. "Let's take a look. We can take you to the hospital if you like."

She shook her head, her mascara smeared with tears. "I'm okay. What will happen to him?"

Gabe was gentle and soothing with the woman. "He's going to spend the night as a guest of the city of Plenty. Do you have a place to stay?"

The woman pointed to a few people who had gathered to watch the altercation. "I'm with them. We're driving back to Tampa tonight."

"You weren't with him?"

She shook her head. "I met him tonight. He seemed pretty harmless when we were negotiating the scene."

Gabe placed the ice pack on the woman's face. "Take some advice. There are a lot of bad Doms out there. Get a reference. Talk to subs who have scened with them before. Samuels is fine when he's sober, but he gets sloppy when he's had too much to drink."

"I will. I'll talk to more people first."

"Good. Are you sure you don't want to see a doctor?"

Her friends joined her, and one put a jacket around the woman's shoulders.

"I'm okay. We're going to head out, I think."

The woman's friends led her to the door and Sami looked at the man she thought she knew.

"You were amazing."

Gabe laughed. "I love that you say that, but I'm not sure how."

Sami shrugged. "The way you handled that guy. Not long ago you would have rearranged his face for him."

Gabe nodded. "Ah, yes, I would have. I haven't handled things like that for a long time. I told you my story today at dinner."

He had told her his story, and she had listened avidly. He'd gone away and ended up staying with a friend from the Army. The friend had introduced him to his therapist and Gabe had started therapy, and eventually found out both the therapist and his Army buddy were in the BDSM lifestyle. Gabe had pursued learning about being a Dominant and it had calmed him down and given him control over his wayward emotions.

The one thing Gabe had not revealed is what he had seen in Iraq that had made him so angry, but Sami hadn't wanted to ask. If Gabe had moved on from it, she didn't want to bring back any bad memories by dredging it all up again.

"I guess seeing was believing."

He brushed back a stray hair and tucked it behind her ear. "Do you believe now?"

She nodded. "Yes. You weren't even close to losing your temper."

He looked every inch the calm and in control Dominant she'd read about in the naughty books she'd borrowed from Sadie. In fact, she'd pictured stripping him out of those leather pants all evening. Her memory carried a vivid picture of what was underneath.

"You can't imagine how much it means to me to hear you say that. I've waited a long time."

She smiled, her heart feeling lighter than it had in a long time. Suddenly, she was filled with hope. "I think you won't have to wait much longer."

Gabe leaned closer so only she could hear him. "I'm looking forward to getting you home, Samantha."

A shiver ran up her spine at the sensual promise in his words. She'd crossed over a barrier with these men today. She wanted to be with them and she was tired of denying her feelings.

Sheriff Ryan strode into the room and clapped his hands on Samuels' shoulders. "Hey, Gabe. I'll take care of this one."

Gabe's slow smile as he gazed at her sent fire licking along her veins. "And I'll take care of this one."

* * * *

Sami kicked off the black jeans and shrugged out of the red button down shirt that was the uniform at Original Sin. She was supposed to meet Jason and Gabe downstairs to tell them her story and she found herself dawdling, trying to put off the inevitable discussion.

She pulled on some sleep shorts and an oversized T-shirt and padded down the stairs, finding Gabe and Jason sitting at the kitchen table working on a cheesecake.

Sami's stomach growled and she realized she hadn't eaten anything since dinner at six. It was now almost two thirty in the morning and she was starved. Jason looked up and grinned, reaching for the cheesecake and cutting her a large slice.

"Don't worry, it's safe. Leah made it."

Leah was Gabe's sister and Jason's cousin and she could cook like a heavenly angel. Sami didn't hesitate to tuck into the creamy confection that practically melted on her tongue.

"This is so good. How is Leah these days?" She licked a stray morsel from her lips and her men instantly zeroed in on her tongue. She fidgeted in her chair, incredibly aware they were also in sleep pants, their chests and feet bare.

Jason's broad chest was almost smooth except for a happy trail on his washboard abs that led down to what she knew was a generously sized cock. Gabe's chest had a light sprinkling of golden hair, not too much and not too little. It made a delicious friction on her nipples when he pulled her close. Gabe's cock was about the same size as Jason's. Maybe a smidge shorter, but slightly beefier in girth. Both had sent her to the stars and back on several occasions.

Gabe swallowed a huge bite with relish. "Did you hear she got married?"

Sami laughed. "Leah finally pulled her nose out of a book long enough to notice the opposite sex? Good for her! Who did she marry and when?"

Jason grinned. "Justin Reynolds and his manager, Linc Davis. They didn't want a big to-do like Ava, so they snuck off to the Keys and got married in a small ceremony in May. Gabe and I attended. It was nice. Justin and Linc are good men. They own the new nightclub, Party Like a Rock Star."

Sami frowned. "Justin Reynolds? Not *the* Justin Reynolds? The rock star?"

Gabe cut himself another slice of cheesecake. "The very same. When Leah does something, she doesn't do it halfway. You should call her and have lunch or something."

"Becca asked me to have dinner at the diner with them on Monday night. Leah's supposed to be there. The club is closed on Monday night, right?"

Gabe nodded and dug into his cheesecake with gusto. She smiled at their hearty appetites. They could eat anything they wanted and never gain an ounce. Sami wished she could say the same, although both Gabe and Jason had told her she was too thin.

"Who's Ava?"

Jason looked confused. "Pardon?"

"You said Leah didn't want a big wedding like Ava. Who's Ava?"

Jealousy tightened Sami's gut. Maybe this was a woman they wanted.

Jason pushed his plate away with a smile and a sigh, patting his stomach. "Ava is fairly new in town. She's Dr. Mark's nurse from Chicago. You met Mark last night. He's Becca's husband. Anyway, she moved down here and pretty quick, Josh Ryder, Brayden Tyler, and Falk O'Neill snatched her up. They're getting married this month. Huge wedding. The men are richer than sin, apparently. Big traders on Wall Street before they came here."

She watched Jason's and Gabe's expression closely but they didn't change when Ava was mentioned. Good.

Sami nodded. "I think I've met Josh. He owns the coffee shop?"

"He does. Brayden and Falk own the Mixed Martial Arts studio," Gabe answered.

"So many new people in town. It's nice." Sami propped her chin in her hands. "The town's changed in so many ways, but it still manages to stay the same. Like Charlie's pizza."

Jason grabbed her hand and looked deeply in her eyes. "Like how we all feel about each other."

She sat back in the chair and gripped the arms. "This is happening so fast. I swore to myself that I wasn't going to do this again." She snorted. "But next thing I knew, you had me living here and broke through all my defenses."

Gabe nodded. "That was our general plan. You should have known that, sweetheart. Gran was in on it as well. She was the one who planted the B and B idea with Becca, and had the house tented so you had to stay with us."

Sami shook her head in amazement. They were all sneaky, but it felt wonderful to be this wanted. She should have known it would be like this, but she'd lost her way when she left Plenty. Ray had a way of twisting her thoughts until she wasn't sure of her own name.

Jason tucked her hair behind her ear. "It's your turn, babe. We're here to listen."

She looked at them sadly. "My story is hard to tell. It's not a happy one like either of yours."

Jason shrugged. "Mine wasn't all that exciting. I never even left Plenty."

"You became the lead deputy. You're in charge when Ryan's not. That's a big deal. I'm proud of you." Sami reached out for his hand and gave it a squeeze.

"I'm proud of you, too." She hastily told Gabe. She didn't want him to feel left out.

Gabe laughed. "I know. I'm proud of me, too. And this meathead, as well."

Jason lifted her fingers to his lips and gently kissed the knuckles. "Take your time. We're not going anywhere."

"This isn't easy."

"Do you want a drink?" Gabe offered.

She shook her head. She needed to keep her mind clear. "No, I just need to find a way to do this." She took a deep breath. "When I left Plenty, I was heartbroken. I didn't think we could ever work things out. Looking back, I realize I should have stayed. While things weren't good, they certainly weren't hopeless. I just didn't know to make things right between us."

Gabe stroked her hair soothingly. "It wasn't your job to make things right. I had to fix myself. No one else could do it but me."

"Everything was so screwed up. I got that job offer in Orlando and I just wanted to get away for a while. I never intended to stay away almost three years, though. I thought I would work there for six months maybe. Get some good experience and come back. I was hoping by then, things would be okay. Wasn't that sweet of me? The first sign of trouble in our relationship and I bail, leaving you both holding the bag. I'm not proud of that, I'll tell you."

"You thought I'd slept with another woman," Gabe protested. "Of course you were upset and angry."

Jason blew out a breath slowly. "So that's what did it? Gabe slept with someone else?"

Sami shook her head. "He really didn't, but it was just the excuse I needed to leave. If I'm honest with myself, I was looking for justification. I guess I thought it was too hard. You know, being with you both." Tears welled up in her eyes, and she blinked hard. "Turns out being with you two is one of the easiest things in the world. But I was young and naive and thought I should be happy all the time. Shit, no one is happy all the time."

Jason sat back in his chair. "Were you happy in Orlando? Is that why you stayed away so long?"

Tears she couldn't stop started to fall. "It was absolutely the worst time of my life. I was miserable every day."

"Then why didn't you come back?" Gabe asked incredulously.

She swiped at the tears on her face. "I didn't want to bring danger here to my family and friends. Hell, I've probably done it anyway, but

I had to see Gran and I wanted to come home so badly."

Her voice broke and the sobs she'd been holding in so long came shuddering out. Jason lifted her from the chair and pulled her onto his lap, stroking her back as if she were a child.

"Let it all out, sunshine. Then you can tell us whose ass we need to kick."

She sniffled. "I think you probably need to kick mine. I'm the reason this all happened. I did something so stupid."

"You're not stupid." Jason shook his head. "What did you do?"

She pressed her hands to her face. She couldn't look at them.

"I broke the law."

Chapter Six

Jason looked over Sami's head at Gabe. Gabe was shaking his head in denial and Jason wholeheartedly agreed. Sami wasn't a criminal. Fuck, she even drove the speed limit and never crossed against a traffic light. Jason wouldn't believe she'd broken the law.

"Why don't you tell us the story, sunshine? Start from the beginning. Gabe and I don't care what you've done."

She lifted her head, her full lips trembling, her eyes wide and shiny with tears. Jason's stomach twisted into a knot. He'd loved this woman for years and hated to see her in such distress. Tonight they would lay any of her fears to rest for good.

She nodded. "It all started when I took the job in Orlando. I was in the hotel management training program with four other people. We spent quite a bit of time together and all became friends. One of them was particularly attentive to me. His name was Ray. Ray Campbell. He seemed really nice at first."

At first?

Jason didn't like the way this was going. One look at Gabe's expression said he was feeling the same way. Gabe started to open his mouth to say something but Jason shook his head. Sami needed to do this in her own time. She reached for Gabe's water glass and took a few sips trying to compose herself.

"He asked me out on a date. I guess I wanted to prove how over both of you I was so I went out with him. He was handsome and charming and we continued dating for awhile."

Jason didn't like hearing about another guy but he hadn't been a saint after they broke up either. "Go on. We're listening."

"One day I was working the front desk and he asked if I would hold a package for him. One of his friends was going to come pick it up. I didn't think much about it. We do this all the time for guests. So I did." Her teeth cut deeply in to her bottom lip. "He'd ask me to do that every now and then. It wasn't a big deal, but one day he dropped off the package and Marion was there. She worked the front desk. She told him to shove off and that she wasn't holding his drugs for him."

Sami took a shaky breath. "He was dealing drugs out of the hotel." Her voice was soft and she looked thoroughly ashamed, wringing her hands, her cheeks red.

"I swear I didn't know what he was doing. I had no idea at all." Jason believed her. Sami had been very naive when she'd lived in Plenty. It had been something they loved about her, but it had also been something that frustrated them. It looked like she'd had her rose-colored glasses ripped from her eyes forcibly.

"He came by my apartment later that night and I told him I wasn't going to do that for him anymore." Her head dropped so her hair covered her face. "He got mad. Real mad. He grabbed my hair and threw me against a wall. He said I was as guilty as he was and if I didn't do what he said I would go to jail."

More tears came and Gabe jumped up to grab a box of tissues from the powder room. They waited until the crying jag had subsided all the while rocking her and trying to calm her down. Jason had to restrain himself from hopping up and finding this Ray guy and laying a major hurt on him. He wanted to beat on anyone that dared lay a hand on the woman he loved. If Jason had been there, this guy would have a stump where his arm used to be.

Gabe was standing on the other side of Sami, his arms crossed over his chest and a muscle jumping in his clenched jaw. He patted Sami's shoulder and tucked her long blonde hair back from her tear-streaked face. "Why didn't you call Jason? Or come home? Get away from him?"

Sami blew her nose noisily. "I was afraid. I didn't want to go to jail. Then, we were all laid off a few days later. I got a job at another hotel pretty quickly but Ray found me. He threatened to tell the police if I didn't give him money. He said he'd blame everything on me and he'd get immunity for testifying against me."

Jason doubted very much anything like that would have happened, but Sami had little knowledge of the justice system. He wished again she would have called him.

She shuddered. "I kept giving him money and sometimes he was okay. Other times he would knock me around. The funny thing was he never lost his temper. He'd back hand me as cool as you please. Then he'd tell me I shouldn't have drove him to it. He convinced me it was my fault and that no one here in Plenty would help me. Eventually, I got fired from my hotel job because he kept coming around and harassing me and everyone there. My jobs kept getting worse and worse. He wouldn't leave me alone."

Gabe shook his head. "Typical mindfuck. I've seen it dozens of times with asshole wannabe Doms. They isolate a sub then convince her they're the only ones who truly understand her. They're the only ones who care. He sounds like a real asshole."

Sami nodded. "That's how it was. After a few months he wasn't interested in dating me anymore. He only seemed to want to scare me, own me, keep me connected to him in some way. I moved a couple of times and he would find me. I tried to keep my phone number or new place of employment a secret but he would find me and cause trouble."

"Violence against women is a control issue," Jason stated. "I bet he was charming, wasn't he? He probably convinced one of your friends you'd had a lover's quarrel and he needed your new address so you could work it out."

Sami's eyes were wide. "He was charming but scary. He would tell me if I ran away he would find me and hurt my friends and family. I didn't want anyone to hurt Gran. I couldn't let anything happen to her because I made stupid decisions." More tears started to fall and Jason held her tighter, trying to take away the pain.

Gabe sat in the chair next to Sami's. "Did he continue to make you do illegal things?"

She shook her head. "He said as long as I behaved and gave him money, I wouldn't have to do that. He's going to be so angry when he finds out I've left Orlando. My roommate, Sadie, said she'd tell him I was visiting friends and would be back soon, but not tell him where." She scrubbed at her eyes with a tissue. "It doesn't matter if she tells him or not. Eventually, he'll figure out I'm here. When we first started dating, I told him I was from Plenty. I'm terrified he's going to show up here and hurt Gran. That's why I've stayed away. I had to keep her safe!" Sami's head drooped on his shoulder. She was exhausted from the emotional upheaval.

Gabe lifted her chin. "Listen to me, Samantha. No one is going to hurt you or Gran or anyone else. His reign of terror is over. If he shows up in this town, I know about a dozen good old Florida boys that would be happy to show him how we treat people who abuse women."

"I broke the law." Her voice was a mere whisper.

"You didn't know what was going on, honey." Jason assured her. "He used your naiveté against you. He played on your innocence and abused you until you were scared. He's the criminal, not you. He would never have gotten away with blaming everything on you. You have to trust me on this."

"I do trust you. Both of you. When I came here…it was just so nice. Everyone was happy and I didn't want to leave. I didn't want to go back there. I kept telling myself I should but then I wanted to find a way to stay."

"You're staying," Jason said firmly. "You're not going anywhere. The rest of our lives start now."

Jason was horrified at Sami's story. She'd suffered so much since she'd left Plenty and it explained the more mature but haunted look he'd seen in her eyes. He vowed then and there to do everything in his power to make her happy, truly happy, again. She would never be the young, naive girl from a small town he had loved, but she could become the wise woman he would spend the rest of his life with, God willing.

He was startled when she pressed her lips to his. "Please. I need you. Both of you."

He glanced at Gabe and saw the doubt in his eyes. "Sweetheart, you've just been through something really emotional. We can wait for another time."

She turned and grabbed Gabe's hand. "No, I need you. I need to feel alive. I need to feel pleasure and happiness. I haven't felt that since I left. I'm tired of waiting. I feel like I haven't even been living these last two years. I've been half alive, just trying to exist hand to mouth. I want to feel good about myself again. I always felt beautiful when we made love."

Gabe quirked an eyebrow. "We made you feel beautiful? You seemed awful nervous and prone to cover up before. You didn't even like to make love with the lights on."

"I was shy." Sami's simple statement made Jason smile. She had been shy, although she had nothing to be ashamed of. He couldn't get enough of her violet eyes, her satin skin, and her long blonde hair. Her curves had been generous and he'd loved to run his hands down her body, watching her eyes turning almost dark purple with passion.

"You were shy, huh?" Jason kissed her temple. "Are you still shy? Do you want us as much as we want you? Not like three kids, but like adults? Are you a woman ready to love her men?"

A smile spread over Sami's face. "I am. Please take me upstairs. I need to love you both."

Jason stood up, still holding her in his arms. "Yes, ma'am. One night of pure love, coming up. Gabe, turn out the lights behind us. We have a woman to dazzle. She's come home."

Tonight they would make her feel like a goddess, and she would never leave them again.

* * * *

It felt like coming home. They carried her up the stairs and into the bedroom before stripping off her clothes, tossing them carelessly aside. Gabe had reached for the light but she shook her head. It would be different this time. She wouldn't allow her own insecurities about her body to enter their bedroom. This time she would be wild and wanton. A woman who could give and receive pleasure without guilt or embarrassment.

She pushed to her knees on the bed reaching for the waistband of Jason's sleep shorts. Her mouth was already watering at the thought of getting their cocks in her mouth, albeit one at a time. Jason's hand covered hers and within seconds he was kicking the shorts away, standing in front of like a Michelangelo statue. Every inch of him was muscle and her fingers were drawn to a new tattoo on his right abdomen. She traced the intricate design, in awe of the vivid colors. She looked up into his soft blue eyes.

"It's beautiful."

"It's a phoenix." Her brows knitted. "The phoenix rises from the ashes and is born again. Just like our love."

She smiled up at him. "I've never seen a phoenix before so I'll take your incredibly romantic word for it."

She beckoned to Gabe. "You're overdressed for the occasion."

Before she could tug his pants down, he quickly shucked them tossing them high into the air so they could land on the dresser. His body was more muscular than she remembered, his abs flat and ridged, his shoulders massive.

"Talented," she smirked.

"That's not all I can do." He rolled his eyes at Jason. "Although I don't have the soul of a poet like lover boy here. I'm just a regular guy."

"I don't know about that. I've heard you quote poetry before,"

Sami teased.

Jason groaned. "It doesn't count if it starts out 'There once was a girl from Nantucket.'"

Sami giggled and it felt wonderful to feel this happy and carefree. "I don't suppose it does." She turned back to Gabe. "He's got a romantic tattoo. What do you have?"

Gabe's eyes lit up playfully. He crossed his palms over his heart as if he was going to recite the sweetest sonnet. "I have a poem for you. 'Roses are red, yellow's for ducks. Get on your knees, then you'll get fu—"

"Stop!" Sami held up her hand and rolled on the bed laughing. She'd forgotten what a cut up Gabe could be when he was in a playful mood. Jason watched them with his usual amused tolerance. He'd always been the serious one. Although neither one of them seemed all that serious standing in front of her, butt naked, cocks hard, trying to one up the other in the romance department.

Neither one of them had ever been champions in the romance department. Jason's idea of romance was to take her fishing and Gabe thought there was nothing more romantic than a ride on his cycle. But they'd shown their love in a million different ways. She'd never needed flowers and champagne.

Jason surprised her by coming down on the bed beside her, caging her in with his arms and capturing her lips in a kiss so carnal and deep it took her breath away. He kissed his way across her jaw and started nibbling in her ear as she felt her legs being pushed apart and Gabe's rough cheek brush her inner thigh. She shivered as his hot breath blew across her clit the same second as Jason bit down on a sensitive spot at the base of her neck. She moaned in response and it only served to entice them to tease her more. Their mouths and tongues everywhere but where she wanted them most.

Gabe's tongue trailed over her lower belly as Jason's mouth kissed a wet trail to her already puckered nipples. He lapped at them, his tongue rough, then sucked the nub, pulling on it and sending a frisson of arousal straight to her pussy. She moved her hips restlessly and Gabe pressed her back to the mattress, his upper body pushing her legs even further apart so she was completely on display to his hungry gaze.

"This pussy is so pink and pretty. All wet and ready for my mouth."

He bent his head and went to work on her cunt with his tongue, running it all over before swiping at her clit. She gave a strangled groan, her body tensed for release as they gave her more pleasure than she'd ever remembered receiving. When her orgasm came, it took her over the edge, her body vibrating and pulsing, the lights dancing in front of her eyes. It seemed endless but eventually she came floating back to earth, her eyes fluttering open to find two grinning men watching her.

She'd never been known for her decorum and maturity in the past, and couldn't stop herself from sticking her tongue out at them. They both smiled and chuckled, Gabe pulling himself up until his large cock bobbed in front of her face.

"I can think of something better for that cute, pink tongue." He waggled his eyebrows.

She smiled and propped herself up with her elbows and licked at the reddish-purple head of his cock, flicking the slit where a pearly drop of pre-cum awaited her. She leaned forward and engulfed the head of his cock in her mouth drawing a ragged moan from Gabe, his fingers winding in her hair, locking her in place. She didn't want to pull off, his cock pushing to the back of her throat, her tongue rubbing all the ridges and making him shudder.

Jason came around to her back, pressing her up to a sitting position so she was reclining on him, his fingers plucking and twisting her aching nipples. Jason remembered she liked it on the rough side. He nuzzled her neck and nipped at her shoulders while he urged her on.

"That's it, sunshine. Suck Gabe hard like a good girl."

Gabe loved getting blown and she knew just what he liked. She hollowed out her cheeks and took him as far as she could, swallowing on him. He bit off an expletive, his fingers tightening in her hair. She reached up and stroked his balls and his cock swelled in her mouth. Jets of hot cum shot to the back of her throat and she had to swallow frantically not to miss anything. When he was done she licked him until he sat back on his haunches, his eyes closed in satisfaction. He finally opened them, a smile playing on his lips.

"A job well done, sweetheart. You still have a lethal mouth."

She fluttered her eyelashes at his compliment. "I'm glad I haven't lost my touch. The last time I did that was, well, with you."

Gabe sat up, his expression one of surprise. "You didn't sleep with, I mean you... Oh shit, you know what I'm trying to say."

She shook her head. "I didn't date him very long. I just couldn't sleep with him. I still loved both of you. Dating was one thing, but sex was a whole different thing. He got mad, but I wouldn't do it."

Jason tipped her chin up and kissed her hard. "I didn't expect you to do that, but I don't mind admitting I'm glad. I'm a possessive asshole like that."

She cupped his unshaven jaw, loving the feel of the stubble under her hand. "I love your possessiveness. I think it's hot."

Gabe chuckled. "Then you're going to think we're positively irresistible. I'm feeling pretty cavemanish when it comes to you."

Jason's expression was troubled. "Sunshine, while we were apart—"

She shook her head. It didn't matter what went on while she was gone. It truly didn't matter to her. "The only thing that matters is that we're together now. If it hadn't been for both of you, we wouldn't be here at this moment. I would never have had the courage to give us another chance. Besides, I was the one who bailed on us first."

Jason pressed her back into the mattress. "I want to be deep inside you. Do you want that? Do you want me?"

She nodded, her body humming at his hoarsely declared words.

He rummaged in the nightstand and pulled out a condom, rolling it on his impressive cock before positioning himself between her legs. His gaze never left her the entire time, his eyes dark blue with passion.

"It's been too long, sunshine." He hooked his arms under her knees and spread her wide as his cock pressed at her cunt. She was drenched from her orgasm but she still had to catch her breath as he stretched her pussy wide. She grabbed his shoulders, panting for breath.

"Easy. Just give me a minute."

He stilled for a moment and bent his head to kiss and lick her neck and shoulder. The sensations sent arrows of pleasure through her body and she dug her fingers into his biceps.

"More. I'm ready for more."

He gave it to her. He pushed relentlessly inside her until he was into the hilt. He didn't even pause but started a slow and steady rhythm that sent her on the path to release once again. Each thrust of his cock in her needy pussy stroked her clit and soon she was thrashing her head back and forth on the pillow and begging him to fuck her harder. She needed to come desperately, but Jason didn't seem in any hurry.

"Harder. I need it harder. Faster." Her voice was raspy with desire but Jason seemed to understand her urgency. He began to speed up, his cock pistoning in and out of her until she screamed his name. Her body tumbled, rolling in the stars. Wave after wave of pleasure ran through her, stronger than any vibrator could ever get her off.

Jason thrust one last time, his head thrown back in passion, the veins of his neck in sharp relief. He groaned as he came, his breath ragged, his body covered in a fine sheen of sweat. He relaxed on top of her, his breathing slowing, his hands taking most of his weight. Even in the aftermath of lovemaking, Jason was always aware of his size. He was a big man and could easily squash her with his weight.

Eventually, he pulled away and padded to the bathroom to take care of the condom. Gabe stretched out next to her, cuddling her close.

"I admit I never thought we'd all be together like this again. I never thought you'd give me another chance, Samantha."

"I couldn't fathom it either until I came here, but I never stopped thinking about both of you. I stopped being angry at you a long time ago. After what I've seen, your anger issues seem fairly inconsequential. Although I'm glad you have it under control."

She looked up into his face in the dim light of dawn. "I wasn't sure what it would be like with you now."

He stroked her hair softly. "I'm not sure what you mean."

"You're a Dom now. I thought you might try and tie me up or something. Spank me. I just wasn't sure."

He smiled. "I trained to be a Dom to learn about controlling myself. Although it was mainly therapy and meditation that helped me. I don't have a deep-seated need to dominate a woman. I enjoy and I do get sexual satisfaction from it, but I don't crave it as others do. Besides, you don't seem all that submissive to me. Do you disagree?"

"I'm not sure. The idea of being tied up and, well, spanked, does intrigue me. I was thinking about it more day-to-day than sexual actually."

Gabe propped himself up on his elbow. "You mean a power exchange of some sort? How do you know about that?"

"You have an internet connection and I can do a web search. When I saw the club, let's say I did some research. I saw that there are relationships where the Dominant makes all the decisions. I was thinking that might be a good idea."

"You want me to make your decisions for you?" Gabe frowned. "Why would you want that?"

She shrugged, uncomfortable with admitting her inadequacy. "While we were apart I seemed to make one bad decision after another. You and Jason made good decisions. Your lives are much better. I was thinking maybe I should just let both of you make all my decisions for me. It might be safer."

Gabe shook his head. "It doesn't work that way. Safety is overrated, first of all. You need to learn to make good decisions for yourself. You need that confidence. Jason and I will always be here to advise you, but ultimately you need to be in charge of your own life."

She sighed. "I hate it when you're right."

Jason plopped down on the bed on her other side. "Gabe's right about something? I guess it was bound to happen."

Gabe laughed and pointed to Jason. "Asshole. I ought to kick your ass right now."

Sami groaned. This baiting and bickering could go on all night. "I'm still hungry. Can one of you go down and get me some more cheesecake?"

Jason blew a raspberry on her stomach making her giggle. ""We'll all go down for cheesecake. I've worked up quite an appetite." He glanced at the clock. "Looks like that's what I'll be eating for breakfast. I have a shift in a couple of hours. What are you two going to do today?"

"After we catch some sleep, I was thinking we'd head over to the B and B and put in a few hours there. There's a lot to be done," Gabe said.

"I have a haircut appointment with Becca today," Sami remembered. "But I do want to work on the B and B. Maybe we can paint the kitchen today."

Jason nodded in approval. "Sounds like a plan. How about I pick you up after my shift and we eat at the diner for dinner?"

Jason scooped her up, sheets and all, and started carrying her to the kitchen. It was a cozy, domestic scene and it made Sami's feel warm and loved. She had her two men back and she was going to get her life back, too.

Chapter Seven

"Can you just shape it up a bit? I feel like a shaggy dog." Sami pulled at her long hair and made a face.

Becca combed through Sami's hair, pursing her lips in thought. "If we layer it a bit, it will take some of the heaviness away. When was the last time your hair was cut?"

Sami didn't want to admit she'd been so broke she'd taken to trimming her own hair so she shrugged with what she hoped was a careless air. "I don't remember. I guess it's been awhile."

Becca was muttering to herself. "Whoever did it should be forced to get a poodle perm."

Becca started sectioning Sami's hair and trimming the back. "So how's the job at Original Sin? Is it going okay working with Gabe?"

Sami felt her face get warm and Becca's face broke into a delighted grin. "You sly dog. Are you, Gabe, and Jason back together? Please say yes!"

Sami smiled. "Yes. We've decided to give things another try."

Becca let out a whoop that was so loud even the people in the back singing karaoke paused. Her father Mike had put a karaoke machine in the back of her salon when she'd opened it and it was popular with friends and customers. She slapped a hand over her mouth and giggled.

"Shit, I guess I should calm down, but I'm so happy for you. I can only hope the three of you will be as happy as Mark and Travis have made me."

Becca let out a blissful sigh. "Tell me every dirty detail. Hold on, maybe you should wait until Monday night at the diner and tell everyone at the same time. No, wait, I'll never be able to wait that long. Talk, woman."

Same old Becca. It felt wonderful to be back in Plenty again. She never wanted to leave again, even if it was for only a few days. She loved this town.

"I don't know what to say. We talked everything through. We all admitted what we could have done better in the past. We've decided to forgive and move on. Start again, you know. I missed them so much."

Sami deliberately left out the story about Ray. She didn't want to rehash it. She felt too happy. Eventually, she'd have to have a frank discussion with her men about what they would do if Ray showed up here. For now, she felt safe. She'd paid Ray money only a few weeks ago.

"We missed you." Becca looked around the salon and moved closer to Sami. "What's it like with a Dom? Does he order you around?" Becca whispered.

Sami bubbled with laughter. "Gabe likes to order everyone around. So does Jason, for that matter. It doesn't mean I listen to them. It was just regular sex. Gabe says he doesn't have to be dominant all the time."

Becca cocked her head. "What do you want?"

Sami chewed on her lower lip. "I'm not sure. The dominant stuff is kind of hot, but I don't know how I would really like being a submissive. I watched some people play at the club and some of it was pretty out there. I don't want to be set on fire."

"Neither would I. We had fun the few times we played. Very low key stuff. Just some bondage and a little spanking." She giggled. "It keeps a marriage spicy."

The bell over the door rang and a pretty, petite woman with long, dark hair walked in with a big smile and a thick file folder. Becca waved at the newcomer.

"Hey, Ava. Come meet Samantha." Becca gestured to Ava.

"Ava's marrying Josh, Falk, and Brayden very soon."

"Congratulations. You must be very excited." Sami held out her hand and the woman shook it with a welcoming smile before collapsing into a chair and groaning.

"Thank you. I am excited, but mostly exhausted. I've been running around on my one day off trying to get some of this last minute stuff done for the wedding. My feet are killing me."

Ava was wearing a pair of obviously expensive killer heels. Sami would have loved to have a pair of shoes like that but they probably cost a month's pay or more.

"That's because you wear those super high heels," Becca said cheerfully. "I know I say this all the time, but I'm going to say it again. I have no clue how you wear those shoes. I'd have broken my damn neck."

Ava smiled and held out her foot. "Falk bought me these on our last trip to Chicago. Aren't they awesome?"

Becca shook her head. "Falk, huh? He has expensive taste. I bet you could feed a small country for what those cost."

Ava blushed. "He wouldn't take no for an answer. He said if I loved him I would take the shoes."

Sami laughed. "As long as he can afford them, I think there's probably no harm. And since when, Becca, have you become so practical? I remember you had a wardrobe so large your Dad had to build you a second closet."

"Those were the days," Becca snorted. "Now I'm a mom and there's no point in wearing anything expensive that's going to get peed, pooped, or thrown up on. Just wait." She pointed to Ava. "When you get pregnant, all those high heels will end up in storage. You'll wear comfortable shoes like I do." Becca pointed to her athletic shoes.

Ava made a face. "We'll see. Whatever you do, don't mention babies around the guys. We're not even married yet and they're bugging me to get pregnant. Brayden is already talking about designing a princess nursery."

Sami rolled her eyes. "Becca would have loved a room like that when we were kids."

"Heck, I still would." Becca laughed. "So what wedding thing are you working on today?"

Ava pulled a couple of pieces of paper from the thick folder and handed them to Becca and Sami.

"These are the menu cards for the reception. What do you think?"

"They're beautiful," Sami breathed. The cards were a thick creamy heavyweight paper with gold and pink roses in the corner and gold lettering.

Ava smiled, obviously pleased with the compliment. "Thank you. I hope you can make it to the wedding, Samantha. The whole town is invited. My boys wanted a huge wedding, and they pretty much get everything they want."

"The whole town?" Sami wondered what venue would be large enough to hold an entire town.

"I don't think everyone's going to come but we did invite them."

Becca picked up a round brush and a blow dryer. "She's going. She's with Jason and Gabe."

Ava's eye lit up. "Lucky girl. We went to Original Sin about a month back for one of Gabe's classes—Spanking for Fun was the title, I believe. Boy, did my guys love the practice lessons." She glanced at her watch and frowned. "I must fly. We have one more tasting with the caterer from Orlando. But I wanted you to see the menu cards. I'll see you on Monday night. Nice meeting you, Samantha!"

Ava was gone as quickly as she came in. Becca efficiently blow dried Sami's hair, whirling her around in the chair.

"Ta-da! What do you think?"

Sami fingered her hair incredulously. It was soft and silky but with body and wave. It hung down her back in a curtain and Sami was almost speechless.

"I've taken your breath away." Becca grinned. "My work here is done. Go dazzle your men with your beauty."

"I feel bad, Becca. I'm heading to the B and B to paint the kitchen. I feel like I should be attending a ball or something."

Becca removed the cape with a flourish. "You'll be the best looking painter in Plenty."

Sami pulled her wallet from her purse but Becca held her hand up. "Hell no. I'm not taking your money for something I was itching to do anyway."

"I've made plenty of money in tips at the club. Please let me pay you," Sami protested.

"No way. I'm not taking it. Just promise me you'll stay in Plenty."

Sami gave up. She'd seen that look on Becca's face before. "I promise. I don't want to go anywhere ever again."

Becca laughed. "Don't say that. We have to go on our yearly Christmas shopping trip to Tampa now that you're home."

"It's not even Halloween."

"That's right and I bet you don't have a costume yet. You better get to it. They have the party at the new nightclub Party Like A Rock Star and it's a big damn deal. You don't want to miss it."

Sami remembered past parties that had been pretty wild. "I'll work on my costume. I don't want to miss it. Thank you so much. I love my hair. You're an artist. I need to meet Gabe at the house. Call me, okay?"

"I'll call you tomorrow to see how the B and B is coming. Maybe I can stop by and help. I'm decent with a paint brush."

"Be careful what you offer or we'll put you to work." Sami laughed as she headed down Main Street enjoying the sunshine. She had a great haircut and two hot men.

Things were looking up.

* * * *

"It stinks in here." Sami wrinkled her nose. "On the bright side, the kitchen looks fantastic."

They'd painted the kitchen walls a soft yellow and the cabinets, built to last in solid oak, a bright white. It gave the kitchen a clean and sunny feel it hadn't had in many years. Paired with the refinished wood floors and the new appliances Gabe had delivered the day before, the room looked positively gourmet.

Gabe chuckled and started gathering up their supplies. They'd worked hard all afternoon and they had an evening at the club still ahead.

"Paint can be stinky. Luckily, this is a mild time of year. We can leave the windows open tonight and let the place air out a little. It's not supposed to rain for a few days."

Sami leaned down to gather up the tarps and groaned as she straightened up. "I think I overdid today. I haven't painted in years."

Gabe frowned. "Maybe you should take it easy tonight. Soak in a hot tub and let Jason rub some ointment on those sore muscles."

She wadded the plastic tarps up and tossed them in the trash can. "I have a shift tonight remember, boss?"

He pulled her close, his warm body waking up every nerve ending in her skin. "You can call me *Sir*." He pressed his lips to hers and she wrapped her arms around his neck, letting his tongue rub sensuously against hers. By the time they pulled apart, her arousal was revving like the engine on Gabe's Harley. He gave her a playful smack on the bottom sending a frisson of pleasure straight to her cunt.

"Take tonight off. It's a Thursday and that's always a slow night. Friday and Saturday we'll be packed. I'd rather have you at one hundred percent then."

She shook her head. He didn't realize how hard she'd had to work these last few years. She hadn't had many days off and often pulled double shifts for days on end to be able to have money to live and money for Ray. "I just need a shower and a catnap. I'll be raring to go. *Sir*."

He grinned at the emphasis she placed on the title. "If you know how much calling me that turned me on, you'd run screaming from this house and down the street."

She glanced below his belt at the obvious erection pressing against the zipper of his jeans.

"I think I know and I'm not scared at all, Sir." She stepped forward until she was standing right in front of him, his masculine scent teasing her nostrils and making her nipples hard and tight. "In fact, I think I saw a few things at the club the other night I bet you would like." She dropped to her knees in front of him and bowed her head. She was shocked when he immediately hauled her up so she was on her feet again.

"No," he said firmly. "You're not ready to submit. Not for real. We can play if you want. I'll tie you down and I'll spank you, but just in fun. No kneeling, no rules. Just fun."

She ran her hands up his chest. "You never spanked me before. How come?"

He pulled her close and nipped at her ear. "You always seemed so naive. Kind of innocent. We weren't sure how you would react if we turned you over our knee."

"I would have liked it."

He chuckled, the sounds rumbling in his chest. "We'll have to see about that, won't we? Are you asking me for a spanking or just thinking about it?"

She gathered all her courage. "I'm asking for it. I think."

"You don't sound too sure, babe." Gabe reached down and popped open the snap on her shorts. "Maybe we should just see where the mood takes us and go from there."

She was all on board for that. It would be nice to have some time with Gabe, just the two of them. She would make sure she and Jason did the same.

She slid her hands under Gabe's T-shirt and pushed it up, revealing his muscular chest and his flat abdomen. "If we're talking about mood, I'm in the mood to get naked. You have on too many clothes."

Gabe pulled his shirt over his head tossing it away and pushed his jeans down his legs. He paused as he was about to kick them away.

"What is this, a strip show? Get naked, woman."

She giggled and slid her shorts and panties off, followed by her tank top and bra. She looked around the freshly painted room and waggled her eyebrows at Gabe. "Are we planning to christen this room or go someplace more comfortable?"

His answer was to lift her off her feet and place her gently on the large oak kitchen table, insinuating himself between her thighs. He ran his callused hands up and down her torso before cupping her breasts, his thumbs brushing the hardening nipples. She arched into the caress, letting her head fall back and her lids close. She wanted to savor the sensations Gabe stirred inside of her and she wanted him to fuck her now. She wasn't sure which side of her was going to win this battle.

Sami moaned as his mouth closed over a nipple, his teeth scraping the sides. Her pussy clenched, wanting him inside. She wrapped her legs around his waist so the hardness of his cock rubbed her swollen clit. Gabe seemed to want to take his time, but she wanted to be fucked now. She clutched the back of his head, as his lips wandered to her other nipple, his fingers pinching the wet nub he'd just abandoned. He lifted his head, giving her a wicked smile. His hand drifted down her torso and slid into her wet pussy and tickling her clit.

"I love this about you, Samantha. You're always ready for me."

He pressed a wet kiss to her abdomen and she spread her legs wide, knowing exactly where he was heading. She braced herself on the table with her hands in back of her as his tongue licked her clit exactly at the same time his thick finger pushed inside of her.

"So tight and hot." He pressed a second finger inside of her. "Tighten up on me, babe. Show me how you like this."

She squeezed her muscles as he began to flick his tongue over her clit and lightly rub her sweet spot. The double sensation almost sent her over the edge and she fell back on her elbows, her arms like limp spaghetti. She tugged at his hair.

"Now. Fuck me now, Gabe," she panted.

He kissed her inner thigh and fished in the pocket of his discarded jeans before holding up a condom in triumph. She giggled and beckoned to him, taking the package from him and tearing open the wrapper with her teeth. She rolled the condom on his cock and she heard his indrawn breath as her fingers brushed the sensitive skin of his balls.

He impaled her in one stroke, driving deep inside. She dug her nails into his back as he rode her hard and fast, each thrust rubbing her clit and sending her closer to heaven. Their breathing was ragged and she let her head fall back so her neck was exposed for his lips. He took the hint and nipped and licked at the flesh sending her on a frenzied spiral of sensation. Her climax uncoiled from her belly and sent waved and sparks to her extremities and curled her toes with its intensity.

Gabe roared his completion moments after hers, his body tensing, his expression stamped with passion. They both lay there, catching their breath and letting their heartbeat slow to normal. She winced as he drew away and he kissed the top of her nose before heading to dispose of the condom. She snagged her clothes from the kitchen floor, getting dressed on wobbly legs. Gabe playfully scowled when he returned.

"You weren't supposed to get dressed. You're supposed to stay naked for me all of the time."

Sami laughed and grabbed two sodas from the refrigerator. She was parched after all the activity.

"We have things to do. I want to grab a nap and dinner before tonight." She handed him a can of soda and saw he'd pulled his jeans on but left his shirt off. He tugged her in close and nuzzled her ear.

"I didn't hurt you did I, babe? You seemed sore when I pulled out."

She shook her head, pulling him back for a kiss. "I'm fine. We just went at it pretty hard. It felt amazing, so no worries."

"Next time, I'll take it slow and easy," he grinned.

"The hell you will. I like it fast and hard. Don't go treating me like a china doll. I'm a grown woman and I know what I like."

"I've noticed, Samantha. You've really grown up since you left Plenty."

"I didn't have much choice," Sami said wryly. "I couldn't stay naive and survive."

"You should have come home. I wasn't here, but Jason would have taken care of you."

Gabe was frowning now. She smoothed the wrinkles from his forehead. "I didn't think I could come home. I know better now. Next time, I'll know."

"There better not be a next time." Gabe's voice was loud in the quiet room.

"Calm down." She patted his chest. "I'm not going anywhere. I'm just saying I won't let anyone convince me that I don't have people who care about me."

"Damn straight. Plenty is your home and your family."

"That's why I stayed away. To protect all of you. I'm still worried about bringing trouble here. I don't want anyone to get hurt."

"No one's going to get hurt," Gabe assured her. "It's safe here in Plenty."

Sami wanted to believe that with all her heart.

Chapter Eight

Jason had picked up Gabe and Samantha from the B and B and they were headed to dinner. When he missed the turnoff to the diner, Sami elbowed him in the ribs.

"Hey! You missed the turnoff. Are you daydreaming? I'm hungry."

"We're not going to the diner. We have something different in mind." Jason had a mysterious look on his face. She'd forgotten how much Jason loved surprises. For someone so levelheaded, he was quite spontaneous. She turned to Gabe who also had a smile playing on his lips.

"I don't suppose you're going to tell me where we're going?"

"Nope," Gabe shook his head. "It's a surprise. If I tell you, I'll ruin the surprise."

She sighed and tried to divine their destination from the road signs. By the time she realized were they were going, she was practically bouncing up and down in her seat. Moss Park was not far from Orlando and a great place to camp. She hadn't been in years, the last time with her men.

Gabe laughed at her delight. "I think she's figured it out."

"Wait," she said, a thought occurring to her. "What about Gran's dinner? What about the club?"

Jason waved off her concern. "Relax. I saw Gran before I picked you up and Lacey said she would take her dinner and visit with her tonight. This was Gran's idea, you know."

"And the club will be fine," Gabe assured her. "I told you Thursday is a slow night. I've got Gary managing the front and Sam, one of the monitors managing the back. We'll be back by opening tomorrow night."

Sami sighed happily. "Good. Gran's getting sneakier as she gets older. She's trying to make sure we all three get plenty of time together. She wants us to fall in love again."

Sami wasn't guessing Gran's intentions, she knew them. Gran had come right out and told her she'd tried to convince the men to ensnare her with great sex so she'd stay. At first she'd been shocked, but this was Gran. Gran would do anything to keep Sami in Plenty. Besides, Gran had said it was for Sami's own good. These were the men for her. Sami hadn't argued.

Jason gave her a sidelong glance. "Smart woman, your Gran."

They took the exit to the park and drove back into it until they found their spot. The men hopped out and started to unload the back of the truck. Sami peered at the bags. "Please say you packed me some clean undies for tomorrow."

"Doubt you'll need panties." Jason was grinning ear to ear. "We have plans."

"A toothbrush?" she asked hopefully.

Gabe whistled as he started to build a fire. "You sure are picky. I distinctly remember packing you a bag. It's right there." He pointed to a small duffle bag. She pounced on it, crowing in delight when she found she had not only a toothbrush and panties, but also an entire change of clothes for the next day plus deodorant. She held it up.

"Guess you didn't want me to get stinky, huh?"

Jason pulled three fishing poles from the back of the truck. "Doubt we'd notice how you smelled with the aroma of fish."

Sami groaned. "We're going fishing?"

"Only if you want to eat dinner." Jason laughed.

Sami was starving and both the men knew it. She wearily reached out for one of the poles. "Okay, let's get this over with."

Two hours later, Sami was sitting between Gabe and Jason in front of the campfire, her stomach pleasantly full of grilled fish and vegetables. She was currently working on a s'more but the marshmallow was dripping down her chin. She giggled as Gabe pulled her close and licked at the sweet confection.

She let Jason and Gabe steal bites from her dessert until it was all gone. She sipped at her beer and regarded her men steadily.

"This surprise getaway has been great but I'm beginning to think there's more to it than fishing and toasting marshmallows."

Her men had been preoccupied since they'd arrived and it usually meant they had something on their mind.

Gabe nodded. "We wanted to bring you someplace quiet to talk to you. We know you've wondered what made me so angry when I came home. I'm ready to tell you now. That is, if you still want me to."

Shock ran through Sami. She had come to the conclusion she was never going to hear about Gabe's time in Iraq. It would simply be a secret between them.

"I do, but I thought you didn't want to talk about it again."

Gabe pointed to Jason. "That was my initial plan but this guy convinced me that if I didn't talk about it, it would always be there festering between us. I don't want this to be an obstacle. Let's just clear it away."

Sami wrapped her arms around her legs, pulling them close. There was a part of her that was glad to be hearing this and a part that was scared. She couldn't make these memories go away for Gabe, or Jason either.

Jason cleared his throat. "I'm going first. You always wondered why I didn't come back angry like Gabe did. Shit, it's just not in my nature to be pissed off at the world. But I did come back sad. Sad and grateful. I was sad to see the death and destruction, but grateful to come home and see happiness and peace. I guess you could say that my glass was half full when I came back."

Sami wanted to reach out to Jason and comfort him, feeling a kinship she hadn't felt before. She'd felt the same way when she returned to Plenty. She hadn't seen what he'd seen but she had seen an uglier side of life and people. She'd been grateful to return to a place where fear and desolation wasn't an everyday occurrence.

"Did you see people die?" Sami wasn't sure it was the right question but she needed to know how bad it had been.

Jason's expression was grim. "Yes. Not every day, but yes. I'm still not sure what they did to deserve to die like that. You know they say war is hell. The fighting is hell but what's really hell is trying to make sense of why someone is allowed to die so far away from the people they love. Even if you hate someone, I don't think they should have to die that way." He shrugged, his face shrouded by the light from the campfire. "I was luckier than most. I saw good things. People who cared about one another." He took a deep breath. "I was glad to come home. Life is simpler here. I don't have to worry every day about being shot by a sniper or blown up by a roadside bomb."

He poked at the fire with a stick, looking into the flames. "So that's why I wasn't angry. I was grateful."

Sami swallowed hard. "I'm grateful you came back in one piece."

He finally looked at her with a small smile. "Me, too, sunshine. Thoughts of you and this town are what got me through some dark moments."

They were all quiet for awhile until Gabe stood. "I said I didn't want to talk about this again, but I'm going to, just once more." Gabe stared up at the moon. "I saw many of the same things Jason did. We were scared every fucking day. We were supposed to be flushing rebels out of Fallujah. You'd get rid of one and two more would take their place. Our unit was a tight group of guys. You really get to know one another in those conditions. Shit, most of us were pretty young, some no more than kids really. They assigned our unit to escort a convoy of supply trucks. Everything was going pretty good then we were ambushed. Guns and bombs everywhere. One of the guys, Mike Johnson, was hit bad. Mike was younger than me but already had a wife and a kid on the way. He'd enlisted to get a steady paycheck and health insurance for his family. Can you fucking believe that? Instead he got himself shot."

Gabe started to pace. "I crawled on my belly to get to Mike but it was too late. He died in my arms talking about his wife and baby. He was going to have a son." Gabe stopped and swung around, his face a mask of pain. "Why did I live in that ambush and he died? He had a wife and a baby to go home to. He should have lived. The randomness of it all, the lack of fairness drove me crazy. When I came home I was so fucking angry at the world. I came home and saw a world where everyone had no clue that life could be kind one minute and fuck you the next. I was pissed that I was the only one who could see it."

Sami stood and walked to Gabe, but was too afraid to put her arms around him. "You had people to come home to, Gabe. I was waiting for you to come home. We didn't have a baby on the way, but I loved you."

Gabe reached out and she ran into his arms. "I know. I know, babe. I just couldn't deal with things. So I left and went to see Mike's wife. By then she'd had her baby. I spent some time there and then moved on to see another guy in my unit who saw I needed help." Gabe looked over her shoulder at Jason. "When I came home I apologized to Jason and even let him take a free shot at me. It wasn't fair that I left him holding the bag. It wasn't fair I made him always be the grown up in our triangle. It was time for me to grow the hell up. I hope I have, but I'll spend the rest of my life making it up to both of you. Being angry was an indulgent response. Jason didn't have that luxury."

His arms loosened and she turned to look at Jason who was still staring into the fire. She swiped the back of her hand across her tear-filled eyes. "No, he didn't. I need to apologize, too. I wasn't any better than Gabe. I let you be the mature one while I had the nerve to complain about Gabe being wild. I was just as bad. I didn't take responsibility for anything and when the going got tough, I left." She smiled through her tears. "I guess I could let you take a free shot at me, but I don't take a punch well."

Jason finally looked up. "I'd never hurt you, Samantha Jane. I was pissed at both of you for a long time. It didn't change anything. It didn't make me feel any better. It just made the days and nights longer. After awhile, I was exhausted holding on to it, so I let it go. Thank you for apologizing."

"You're a good man." Sami knelt down next to him.

"I'm no saint," Jason shook his head. "Don't think I didn't curse your names or think horrible thoughts. I did. It even occurred to me to try and push you away when I saw you again. Make you hurt like you hurt me. But in the end, I knew it wouldn't make me feel better. I spent many nights sitting at Leah's kitchen table eating cookies and spilling my guts. She listened for a long time, hell, months and months. Then one day, she said to pick myself up, stop feeling sorry for myself, and move on." Jason smiled. "You know how she is. She doesn't feel sorry for herself and she was done feeling sorry for me."

Gabe chuckled. "I bet she was tougher than any therapist I might have been seeing."

"She kicked my ass, that's for sure. She was right. It was time to stop crying in my beer and live again. So that's what I did."

Jason straightened his legs out and pulled Sami on to his lap. "All this emotion sure wears a man out. Maybe we should hit the sack."

Sami looked from Gabe to Jason and back again. "That's it? You spill your guts and you're done?"

"What else do you want to talk about?" Gabe asked. "We've told you about Iraq. We've all apologized for our part in what happened. What else is there to say?"

She stood, her hands on her hips. Men were idiots and these two took the prize. "There's a lot to say. Like, I love you, okay? Both of you. It's not like it was before. It's different now. Deeper and, well, I don't know, but it feels better. More real. Gabe has become the man I'd always hoped he could be, and Jason is even more of what he was and then some. You make me feel safe. You make me feel happy. Mostly, you just make me feel things, and I haven't felt anything for a really long time."

Jason smiled. "We're declaring our love? I'm in. Gabe, you ornery son of a bitch, I love you like a brother. The brother I never wanted and got anyway. I forgive you for running and I'm glad you're back. This woman is too much trouble to handle alone. She'd run me into an early grave without you." He turned her face so she was looking into his eyes. "Sunshine, I love you. I love the girl you were, and the woman you've become. I thought I needed to keep the innocence in your eyes, but I see now that you need to see the world not be protected from it. I love how you've survived and can still see the good. I love how you see the good in me."

Sami sniffled as she looked up at Gabe. It was all up to him now. He crossed his arms across his chest with a smile. "I'm not a man given to words, as you both know. Actions usually say things better. I let you take a swing at me, Jason, so you know you're my brother and best friend. I never wanted a brother either, you know. I was perfectly happy with one sister." He grinned at Jason then looked at Sami. All she could see was the love he felt. "As for you, Samantha, I do love you. Fuck, I let you take a crop to me. I don't know how to express my love, but it's there. It's always been there, even in my darkest moments. It's what got me through some bad times. The thought of never seeing you again was like a shadow over all the good things." He stepped closer. "I'm proud of you. You went through something that could have broken someone weaker. You didn't fold. You fought and scrapped and came out the other side of it a better person."

Jason was laughing now. "He let you take a crop to his ass? How did I miss this? I would have paid money to see that."

Gabe picked up his beer and took a long drink. "I couldn't crop her ass, she wasn't ready. So I let her crop mine. She barely hit me but I got the reaction I was going for."

Sami remembered she'd broken down into tears. "You did that on purpose? That was mean. I cried."

"You needed to cry," Gabe declared. "You needed to cry badly. If beating on me with a crop helped, then I'm glad I let you."

"When are going to beat on me with a crop?" Sami held her breath as her two men exchanged a glance.

Gabe rubbed his chin. "Are you saying what I think you're saying? You want to play some games with us?"

"You both said you should have spanked me back then. Maybe you should do it now. We are trying to clear the air." Sami watched their reaction closely.

Jason pushed to his feet. "Samantha Jane, if you want a spanking, we're the men to give it to you." She sucked in a breath as he bent over and put his shoulder in her stomach so he could lift her in a fireman's hold. He strode over to the tent and dumped her down on the air mattress he had set up.

"Strip and get ready." He rubbed his hands together. "I can't wait to spank your ass a bright red."

Sami gaped up at him. What the hell had she gotten herself in to? These men were her life and she was theirs. She'd grown up and finally seen them as they truly were. They weren't heroes, perfect in every way, fixing every little thing for her. They were men. Ordinary men who tried and sometimes failed. All three of them didn't always make the best decisions but they'd been given a second chance at love and Sami wasn't going to squander it.

* * * *

Samantha's expression was priceless. Half excited and half "oh shit," she was stripping off her clothes as he and Jason watched. Gabe reached out and squeezed the back closing of her bra before she could reach it and it flicked open with a satisfying pop. Samantha's eyes got big and he grinned.

"Just trying to help."

"I didn't know you could do that."

"It's only two hooks, babe. A child could do that."

She held the bra up in front of her like a shield. "You did it so fast."

"Samantha Jane." Jason shook his head and chuckled. "Drop the brassiere."

Color flew into her cheeks and she drop the bra onto the ground, then tugged her panties down her legs. She stood in front of them, bare to their gazes. She'd never had the courage to do that in the past and Gabe admired her bravado now.

"Beautiful, isn't she, Jason? So damn gorgeous I don't know what I want to kiss first."

She did look beautiful with her long golden hair and her big blue eyes. She was slowly getting her curves back and he savored each line and plane of her body in the low light. Her waist was impossibly tiny and her hips and bottom perfect for a spanking. If she wanted one, he'd be more than happy to give it to her. Just the thought had his cock hard and aching inside his jeans.

"You stay high, I'll go low," Jason said before he fell to his knees and pushed her thighs apart. He had Samantha mewling with pleasure in seconds, his tongue working on her pussy and clit. Gabe positioned behind her, cupping her full breasts and kissing and nipping at her neck and shoulders. He could feel her getting heavy in his arms and knew her knees were turning to jelly. He nodded to the floor and they laid her out like a feast, their mouths devouring her flesh. Her skin was soft and fragrant and he breathed in her sweet scent mixed with the musk of her arousal. It made his cock pulse against his zipper and his balls draw up.

Gabe licked at a taut nipple watching it crinkle even tighter before drawing it into his mouth. He scraped his teeth across one then the other and listened to her keening with pleasure. He kissed his way down her belly and over a hipbone before nudging Jason.

"Trade?"

Jason grinned and Gabe kissed a wet trail to the inside of her thighs then up to her already drenched cunt. His tongue trailed through the folds of her pussy and flicked at her clit. She shuddered in response and more cream landed on his tongue. She tasted like honey and he pressed two fingers inside of her and felt her cunt flutter in response.

He hooked the two fingers and found her sweet spot while he licked at her clit with the flat of his tongue. It was like he'd hit her with a bolt of electricity. Her body stiffened and then she shook and moaned as her orgasm ran through her. He stayed with her until her body went slack before pulling back to look into her eyes.

"I'm going to fuck and spank you now. Is that what you want, Samantha?"

Her eyes were glazed over from her climax but she nodded. "Yes, I want it."

"We will always give you what you need. Let's get her turned over, Jason."

They easily turned her onto her belly and Gabe pulled her back so she was on her hands and knees. Jason ran his fingers through her hair and caressed her jaw.

"Give us a minute to get rid of our clothes and we'll give you what you've been needing."

They shucked their clothes in record time and Gabe caressed the creamy skin of her ass. It was going to be bright red by the time he was done with it.

"This spanking is for all the spankings we didn't give you before because we thought you were too young or wouldn't enjoy it."

He smacked a round ass cheek leaving a red handprint behind. Damn, it looked hot. He smacked her bottom again and she wriggled in response.

His woman liked it.

* * * *

Sami sucked in her breath as the heat from the spanking spread from her bottom directly to her pussy and clit. She hadn't known how much she'd like being spanked but after only Gabe's palm landing twice on her backside, she was going to be begging for it all the time. It was hot and raunchy and she wriggled her bottom to entice him to keep spanking her.

He didn't make her wait, his hand coming down over and over until honey was dripping down her thighs and her entire body was on fire with the conflicting sensations of pleasure and pain.

"She's got a little bit of masochist in her." Gabe rubbed a sore ass cheek and she arched back in to his hand to spur him on. She didn't want him to stop. It felt like her body had woken up and she needed more and more of what he had to offer.

Jason chuckled, a warm sound in the dim light of the tent. "You've got a little sadist in you so it's a match made in heaven."

Gabe's fingers delved into her cunt and she pressed back on his fingers, trying to impale herself deeper. He responded by pulling them out and smacking her bottom again making her moan with pleasure.

"You want your turn? She seems to want more."

Jason bent down to whisper in her ear. "Do you want more, sunshine? Do you want me to take a turn spanking your cute little rear end?"

"More." Her voice was like gravel but he heard her message loud and clear, taking up where Gabe left off. His hand cracked down on her ass cheeks over and over while Gabe's fingers reached under her and found her swollen clit. He barely touched her and she went off like a sparkler in July. Wave after wave ran through her until she slumped on the mattress, spent and panting.

Gabe praised her, running his hands up and down her back. "Good girl, Samantha. That was excellent. I'm so proud of you."

She rolled over on her back and giggled. "What are you proud of? All I did was have an orgasm."

He leaned over her and kissed her long and slow, his tongue playing with her and leaving her breathless. "I'm proud of you because you took your spanking like a big girl. Not everyone could take a good, hard spanking like that. You should be proud of yourself."

When he put it like that, she was kind of proud. She had taken a spanking and without a complaint. She'd liked it way too much to complain, but she wasn't quite ready to admit it yet. She had a feeling he knew anyway how much she liked it. She also liked the warm feeling his praise gave her. She'd always craved approval from these men.

She reached up, running a hand up each of their chests. "I want you both."

Jason grinned. "Sunshine, you have us both. We're all yours."

"No." She shook her head. "I want both of you at the same time."

Both men frowned and exchanged a worried glance. She'd always said no to this particular intimacy in the past. She'd been too shy, too uptight to enjoy it with them, but now she craved it. She wanted to make love to both of them at the same time.

"Now, Samantha," Gabe began. "Are you sure about this? You've never wanted to before."

She lounged back on the blankets enjoying their discomfiture. "I'm sure. I'm very sure. Don't you want to?"

Jason grinned. "Of course we want to. We love you. We just don't want you to feel pressured to do anything you don't want to do."

"I don't feel pressured. I feel ready."

The men exchanged glances again, smiles spreading across their faces. Gabe pointed to the far side of the air mattress. "Then move so I can lie down. Jason can do the honors. There should be lube in my toy bag."

Sami scooted to the side while Gabe grabbed a small leather bag from the far corner of the tent. He held it up. "This is the portable version. The full size version is at the club."

"You were pretty sure of yourself," Sami pouted.

Gabe laughed and pulled out the bottle of lube, tossing the bag aside. "Never leave home unprepared. I was a Boy Scout."

"You were never a Boy Scout."

"I wanted to be a Boy Scout."

Jason groaned and rolled his eyes. "You never wanted to be a Boy Scout. I was a Boy Scout. You had your chance to join with me, but you weren't interested."

Gabe settled himself on the mattress. "There weren't any girls. If there had been girls, I might have joined." Gabe patted his stomach. "Come here, babe. Straddle me so Jason can get into position."

She moved so her thighs were on each side of Gabe's. He started playing with her nipples and she moved restlessly as her arousal started growing again.

"That's it, babe. Concentrate on what I'm doing while Jason does what he needs to do."

Jason came up behind her, kissing her neck and nibbling on her ear before pressing on her back so she was lying on top of Gabe. Gabe never stopped his campaign of distraction even as she felt the cold trickle of lube down the crack of her ass and Jason's thick finger pressing her back hole for entry. She puffed out a breath as the digit breached the tight ring of muscles. She'd heard enough from other women to know to try to relax, but doing it was different than hearing about it. He only had one finger inside her and she already felt full. She couldn't imagine having an entire cock shoved up there.

More lube and then the press of two fingers. Gabe was doing his damndest to distract her but her brain was firmly fixated on her ass and what Jason was doing with his hand. She felt the burn just as she'd been warned and then his fingers began rubbing dark and naughty nerves in her backside and a moan popped out of her mouth before she could stop it.

Gabe patted her bottom. "That's a good girl. Just relax and enjoy it."

It felt good but strange, and she wondered what Gabe would say if he had something up his butt. Before she could ask him, Jason started scissoring his fingers and stretching her until she pressed her forehead into Gabe's chest, concentrating on taking one breath after the other. There was more lube and more fingers but Sami got lost in the sensation. When Jason pulled his fingers from her bottom she mewled in frustration.

"Easy, sunshine. It's time."

She heard the crinkle of the condom, the trickle of more lube, then the head of Jason's cock pressing forward.

"Deep breath," Jason instructed. "Just go limp and let it happen. I'll take this really slow so I don't hurt you."

"Easy for you to say," Sami muttered but she did as he asked, letting Gabe play with her nipples and kiss her lips to take her focus off what was happening behind her. She was surprised when the head of his cock breeched her opening and was lodged tightly inside her ass. Jason's hands were gripping her hips and she heard him curse softly under his breath.

"Don't tighten up on me, sunshine. Relax those muscles."

She forced herself to breath and relax and soon Jason's own breath was coming easier. She must have clamped down on the head of his cock and almost strangled it in her panic.

"I feel full." It was an understatement.

Jason chuckled. "You're about to get even more full. Just relax and let it happen. You don't have to do anything."

It was hard but she did as she asked. He pushed forward slightly, then pulled out a little, before pushing in, just a little further. Each stroke filled her more and more until he was finally seated to the hilt with a grunt. Their bodies were covered with sweat and she was shaking with the maelstrom of sensations she'd never felt before. No one had told her it would feel this good. She tried to move but this time Gabe's fingers clamped down on her hips.

"Easy, honey. Stay still while I saddle up. You're going to be filled to the brim with cock in a minute."

She lifted slightly so Gabe could roll on a condom then slowly lowered herself on his hard cock. She could feel every ridge of his cock as she took him an inch at a time. By the time she'd taken him all, her pussy was stretched wide and her world was starting to tilt on its axis. The pleasure from being so completely filled was dizzying and it only intensified when they started to move. She closed her eyes and savored every thrust of their cock, every stroke on the sweet spots in her pussy and ass until she was consumed with the fire they stoked inside her.

"I need, I need—" She couldn't verbalize what she needed. She only knew she needed more of them, harder and faster, giving her what only they could. Her body was stretched as taut as a bow string waiting for the touch on her clit that would send her over the cliff. When it finally came it was like a bomb had been detonated inside her. She screamed with the intensity of the pleasure, the waves making her shake and shudder. Jason thrust into her, his body stiffening, his cock seeming to swell as it shot hot jets of cum into the condom. Gabe let go a string of filthy words, his eyes closed, his jaw tense. They all lay very still, a tangle of arms and legs covered in sweat and her juices.

Eventually, Jason stirred and carefully pulled from her body, with Gabe following. They wrapped her in blankets and left her alone in the tent for a few minutes only to return with a damp cloth to clean her up. She protested at first, but Gabe simply kissed her to stop her talking. When they were done, they joined her in the sleeping bags, their bodies curled together. No one spoke, but they didn't have to say any words. They all knew something momentous had happened tonight. Love words had been exchanged, stories told, bodies shared. It was a new beginning for the three of them. It was their second chance.

Chapter Nine

"So everything is going great. We repainted all the rooms, the floors are refinished, and we're now waiting on the furniture delivery. While we're doing that, Zach and Chase are working on renovating the bathrooms. I can't wait for you to get out of here so you can see it."

Sami poured Gran some juice at her regular daily visit. It had been almost a week since she and Gabe finished repainting the kitchen and the work on the B and B had gone at a blistering pace.

Gran smiled. "I'm looking forward to that myself. The doctor says at the end of the week I'll get to move to one of those rehabilitation centers, but we don't have one in Plenty. I chose one in Tampa. Fran Davies said she'd come visit me while I'm there so you don't have to worry about making the trip."

Sami shook her head as she rearranged some of the flowers in the vases. She liked to spruce up Gran's room when she visited. "I don't mind the drive to Tampa. I'll visit you every day."

"No, you will not," Gran said firmly. "You're busy with things here. You can come by on the weekends maybe, but not every day. That's too much. That's why I called Fran."

Sami remembered Fran from years ago and knew Gran would be in good hands. Fran was a good woman with several children and grandchildren. She liked to bake cookies and play shuffleboard.

"We'll see. The house is almost done. I'll bring more pictures next time, but they don't do the place justice. Gabe and Jason have worked so hard. I couldn't have done this without them."

"Gabe and Jason seem awfully smiley when they visit me." Gran chuckled. "Seems things are going well between the three of you. Am I wrong?"

Gran wasn't wrong. Things were going very well indeed.

"We're doing okay. It's going to take some time but I think we're on the right road. It's strange but we've all changed so much it's like falling in love with different people. I remember how I loved them before, but how I feel for them now isn't the same. It's deeper. It means…more."

Sami wasn't sure how to describe it but Gran nodded her head in understanding. "You've grown and changed. A woman's love is deeper, more mature as she ages. This is no crush or infatuation you have for those men. This is the real thing. It's something to treasure." Gran placed her wrinkled hand on Sami's. "It's something worth fighting for, child."

Sami's phone started to go off and Gran laughed. "Better answer it. Those newfangled rings are sure loud and annoying."

Normally her ringtone wouldn't be turned up that loud, but with all the work at the B and B it could get too noisy to hear her phone. She was delighted to see it was Trish, her other roommate from Orlando.

"Hey, girl. I haven't heard from you for awhile. How's everything going?"

"Thank God, you answered, Sami." Trish's voice was tremulous and even over the phone, Sami could tell her friend was upset.

"What's going on? What's wrong?" A feeling of foreboding started to creep over Sami. Things had been going too well and she should have known better than to think they'd stay that way.

"It's Sadie. She's in the hospital." Trish sounded like she was trying not to cry. "Ray came here last night while I was at work. I guess he got mad and he beat her up pretty bad."

Sami could hear Trisha crying now. Her own voice wasn't working well and her heart plummeted to her stomach.

"Is–is she going to be okay?" Sami swallowed the lump forming in her throat. Sadie was one of the best friends she'd ever known.

Trisha sniffed a few times before answering. "Yes, but she has to stay in the hospital tonight. She's all upset because she doesn't have any insurance and she's going to miss work tonight. She thinks they'll fire her."

"I'll be right there. Which hospital is she in?" Sami knew what she needed to do and it wasn't sit in Plenty while her friend suffered. Ray would never have knocked Sadie around if he hadn't been looking for Sami.

"Oh, I was hoping you'd say that," Trisha sighed. "I know Sadie wants you here but she won't ask, you know."

Sami knew every well. Ray would probably be lurking around the hospital corridors waiting for Sami to show up and Sadie wouldn't want that to happen. That's why Sadie had taken a beating instead of just telling him where she was. Trish told Sami which hospital and room and Sami hung up, shaking her head. Gran gave her a sharp-eyed look.

"Looks like bad news. A friend?"

Sami dropped a kiss on Gran's cheek and gathered her purse and keys. "Yes. A friend of mine in Orlando was hurt and I need to get to her. I'll probably spend the night there."

Gran grabbed her hand. "Call Gabe and Jason."

"I don't want—"

"Samantha," Gran interrupted sternly. "Call your men. At the very least let them know, but give them a chance to help you through whatever this is. They want to be there for you. You didn't give them a chance before. Give them that chance this time."

Sami hung her head, knowing Gran was right. She'd fled Plenty last time, not willing to talk about anything. She nodded her agreement. "I'll call them. I promise, okay?"

Sami headed down the hall, punching buttons on her phone. She'd call Jason and Gabe, grab a change of clothes, then head to Orlando. What happened to Sadie was all her fault and somehow she needed to make this right.

* * * *

Jason walked next to Sami down the hospital corridor, his nostrils full of the smell of antiseptic. He hated hospitals but wasn't about to let Sami deal with all this alone. She'd insisted she didn't need anyone to accompany her to Orlando, but one look at her shattered expression had told him he needed to be there. Gabe couldn't leave the club, but Ryan had given Jason a few vacation days without any problem.

"This is it. 318." He held the door open so Sami could precede him into the room. His gut tightened into a knot as he spied the lone inhabitant in the room. At first, he thought it was a child, the woman was so small and thin. But now he could see she was an adult, perhaps in her mid-twenties. Her face was battered and bruised, one eye swollen shut, her lips puffy. Her left arm was in a sling and there were a smattering of bruises up and down the exposed skin of her arms and neck. This Ray guy had put a major hurt on this tiny woman. The thought that this could have been Sami made acid rise in his throat. Jason was going to feed this guy his fingers, one by one, then start on his spleen.

Jason saw tears in Sami's eyes as she rushed forward and they awkwardly hugged, the woman obviously in pain. She kept shaking her head in denial. "You shouldn't be here. Ray will find you." She kept saying it over and over again, both of them in tears. Jason hung back, not sure what to say or do to make everything right. He only knew he damn sure wasn't letting this guy get near Sami or her friend ever again. He needed to have a long talk with Ryan when they returned to Plenty. Jason had given him a bare bones sketch of what was going on but they'd agreed Sami needed to come talk to Ryan and put an end to all this once and for all. Ryan had connections with the Feds and heaven knew who else. For once, Jason was glad his boss was a total badass.

Sami brushed her tears away and smiled. "Sadie, this is Jason Carrington. Jason, this is Sadie Stewart."

He shook Sadie's good hand. "It's nice to meet you. Are they treating you well here? Is there anything we can bring you?"

Sadie's eyes welled up again. "I need to get out of here. I can go back to the apartment. I don't have any medical insurance and I'm going to miss work tonight. Harvey is going to fire me."

He patted her hand. "Don't worry about the bill. We'll take care of that. As for your job, I don't think you should worry about that. We're here to take you back to Plenty with us tomorrow morning when they discharge you."

Her eyes went wide. "Leave?" She turned to Sami, clearly panicked at the idea. "Is this your idea? How will I pay my bills if I'm in Plenty? I'll lose the apartment. Trisha can't pay the rent by herself."

Sami calmed Sadie down, holding her hand and sitting next to her on the bed. "We're taking both of you with us. It's not safe here in Orlando. Jason and I discussed this on the drive here. Is there anything to keep you in Orlando? You said you don't have any family and let's face it, all we had here was a crappy job and a shitty place to live. You can get a job in Plenty."

He saw hope light up in the poor girl's eyes. "You're really taking us? Do you think I can get a job in Plenty?"

"What do you do, Sadie?" Jason asked.

She looked up at him and he sat down in a chair so she wouldn't have to crane her neck. She must be sore as hell from a beating like that. "I'm a waitress right now. I used to do some clerical work when I could find it."

"I bet you can work for Gabe," Jason nodded. "He has a club and Sami's working there right now. He's always complaining he can't keep good employees."

Sami rolled her eyes. "For good reason." Sami leaned forward and whispered loudly. "It's a BDSM club. You know like in those books you read."

Sadie looked shocked and then smiled, wincing as she did so. "Shit, that hurt. Note to self. Don't smile or laugh until my lip and ribs heal." Sadie pressed the button that lifted the bed so she was sitting more upright. "Have you talked to Trisha about this? I don't think she'll go. She has family here."

"We haven't talked to her." Sami shook her head. "But we're heading over there tonight to pack up what's left of my stuff and yours, too. We'll talk to her then."

"She's working tonight so she won't be there."

"We'll go by in the morning then." Jason couldn't sit still. He walked over to the window that looked out over downtown Orlando. The city streets below were full of people and traffic. Too much for his small town soul. He didn't know how Sami could stand it. He could only take a big city for a few days. He turned back to Sadie, who looked exhausted. They needed to let her get her rest if she was going to leave with them tomorrow morning.

"Does he know Sami's in Plenty? It's okay if you told him. I just need to warn Gabe and Sheriff Ryan if he does."

"I swear I didn't tell him. He was so mad when he showed up and you weren't there. There was no reasoning with him."

Sami patted Sadie's hand, her expression anguished. Sami was blaming herself and Jason needed to intervene quickly. While she was busy beating herself up over this, she wouldn't be thinking clearly. They all needed to be thinking clearly right about now. Currently, there was a violent asshole out there who didn't care who he hurt to get what he wanted.

They stayed for a little while longer but it was clear Sadie was exhausted from the pain and the medication they were giving her. They left with a promise to pick her up in the morning.

"Should we go to the apartment tonight or tomorrow?" Jason asked as they drove away from the hospital.

Sami checked her watch. "Let's go now. Trisha is a bartender and works the late shift so we might catch her at home before she leaves for work."

"Just point me in the right direction."

Jason didn't know the roads of Orlando well. He knew how to get to Disney and Universal Studios, but that was about it. Sami directed him and with each turn he became more alarmed. By the time they pulled up in front of her apartment building, Jason was sick to his stomach. The woman he loved had been living in what could only be described as a dump in the middle of the worst neighborhood he'd ever seen in person or on television. His hand automatically went to where he normally wore a sidearm and he sighed in frustration when it wasn't there.

No wonder Ray had been able to get away with beating up Sadie. No one would notice in this hellhole. They walked up the stairs and Sami produced a key that to Jason's dismay opened up a flimsy lock on the doorknob. They didn't even have fucking deadbolt. Thank God he was taking the women back to Plenty in the morning. The thought of Sami living like this was horrific.

Sami pushed open the door and the sight greeting them was even more depressing. Faded, torn furniture, and stained carpet was the main decor. A woman rushed to the door from the back of the apartment dressed in short shorts and a tight T-shirt. She ignored him and hugged Sami.

"Sami, I've missed you! You look great! How's your grandmother doing?"

"She's doing fine. Getting better every day. I'm so glad we caught you before you headed to work. We want to talk to you. Do you have a few minutes?"

Trisha grimaced. "Just. As you can see from this ridiculous outfit, I'm bartending tonight. Did you see Sadie?"

Jason and Sami sat down on the worn sofa. "We did," Sami answered. "I told her we're packing up her things and taking her to

Plenty with us. With Ray, out and about, it's not safe to stay here. We want you to come, too. Oh, this is Jason Carrington. Jason, this is Trisha."

After seeing the neighborhood, Jason didn't think it was safe to stay even if Ray wasn't an issue but now wasn't the moment for him to air his opinions. He and Trisha exchanged greetings, but she shook her head in response to Sami.

"I really can't leave Orlando. I have family here. A sister. She's been after me to move in with her but I didn't want to leave you and Sadie in the lurch. I can move in with her now and not feel guilty. Thank you for thinking of me though. Maybe I can visit you sometime?"

"We'd love that. Are you sure? I think you'd really like Plenty."

"I can't." Trisha shook her head sadly. "I can't leave my sister. She's been through too much. She really needs me. I'll miss you though. Promise me you'll keep in touch."

The women hugged and promised to exchange emails and texts which Jason knew was the modern way to communicate. Personally, he preferred to talk to someone face to face. He was old-fashioned that way.

Trisha headed to work and he and Sami started to pack up their belongings. Once again, Jason was struck by the meagerness of what they owned. There was no television, and just a few pots and pans. Both women had some clothes but not many. Now he knew why there wasn't a better lock on the door. There'd been nothing to steal.

"Do we need to inform the landlord you're leaving?"

Jason had to make a concerted effort not to say slumlord. Sami continued packing photos and personal items for Sadie. "No. I've never seen him or her. They have a drop box by the mailboxes. I'll leave them a note. They won't care."

Jason carried the last box and suitcase to his SUV. Sami was standing at the door of the apartment looking at it with a mixture of sadness and disgust.

"I know what you've been thinking. It's truly awful. The apartment, the neighborhood. I guess I got used to it but after being in Plenty even for a few weeks, coming back here…" Sami shuddered and he put his arm around her shoulders pulling her close. "It was all I could afford. I'd sold off everything to keep paying Ray. All three of us were scared but there are really nice people in this neighborhood. They watched out for us."

Jason sent a prayer up to heaven in gratitude that these women had someone who'd been looking out for them. He rubbed her arm in a soothing motion.

"It's over. You're coming home."

"It's not over. Ray's still out there. He'll come after me."

Her eyes were shiny with tears and it tore at Jason's heart. "I'm working on the whole Ray thing. Trust me?"

"I trust you with my life."

Jason helped her into the truck and they drove away. Sami never looked back as they headed down the street toward the freeway. He would make sure she never had to live like this again.

* * * *

"Did you get enough to eat?" Jason asked as he pulled his shirt over his head and carefully folded it back into his suitcase. Much to Sami's relief, he'd insisted they get a hotel room instead of sleeping at her shit hole of an apartment. She'd been mortified when she'd seen his expression. Looking at it through his eyes had been painful, but with some luck it was all behind her. Jason and Gabe had vowed to get Ray off her back. She didn't know how they were going to do it, but felt relieved she had someone on her side.

"I ate enough for two people." Sami grinned and patted her stomach, eyeing Jason's muscular, bare chest. "Are you hot?"

He waggled his eyebrows. "I don't know. What do you think?"

She giggled and made a grab for his arm, tugging him down onto the bed with her. "I think the answer is yes, but that's not what I meant. I was asking if we needed to turn the thermostat down, silly."

"Temperature's fine. I just don't like extra clothes if I don't have to have them. I prefer running around in shorts if the truth be known."

He looked a little embarrassed and Sami couldn't stop herself from teasing him a bit. "Deputy Jason, long arm of the law, doesn't like to wear clothes? He wants to run around naked?"

He lounged back on the bed, his hands behind his head. Sami's gaze was drawn to the flex of his biceps and the ridges on his flat stomach. She had an overwhelming desire to trace his abs with her tongue. She dragged her attention from his muscles and back to his face.

"Maybe I do like being naked. I like it when you're naked."

She sat up and swung her leg over his hips so she was straddling him on the bed, his cock hardening underneath her. "Is that a hint? Are you going somewhere with this conversation?"

He grasped her hips then ran his hands up her ribcage, under her shirt, pulling it over her head and tossing it away. His eyes were dark with passion as he reached behind her to flick her bra open.

"I'm not much for subtlety, sweetheart. How about I say it loud and proud? Let's fool around."

She giggled and helped him fling her bra over her shoulder and off the bed. His large hands were warm as he caressed her breasts, stroking the sensitive skin underneath and teasing the taut nipples with his thumbs.

"I think that's a great idea. You're such a smart man." She pressed her own hands over his, loving the contrast between her own skin and his much rougher skin.

He chuckled and lifted his head while pulling her down closer so his mouth could capture a nipple. She moaned as he worried the nub between his lips and teeth sending flashed of fire directly to her clit and pussy. He rolled her to her back and began working on her jeans and panties, tugging them down her legs and throwing them off the bed where they landed in a heap on the floor.

"Yep, this is how I should keep you. Bare ass naked. But for my eyes only. Mine and Gabe's."

Jason had a wide grin on his face and she reached up to pop the button on his jeans. "Get naked, Deputy. You're lagging behind here."

"Yes ma'am." Jason laughed, clearly pleased she was taking initiative in the bedroom. In the past, she'd pretty much left it to him and Gabe to pursue sex. Now she felt a hunger and drive of her own, much stronger than before. She liked feeling this way and she especially liked that her men were pleased as well.

Jason scooted backward off the bed and slowly pulled the zipper of his jeans down, then teasingly back up. "Are you sure you want me naked, Sami? I think I need to hear you say it."

She didn't hesitate. "I want you naked and on top of me, Jason. I want your tongue and cock in my pussy. I want you."

Her voice was hoarse with the passion that was overwhelming her. She never took her eyes from Jason as he shucked his pants and boxers. He stood proudly before her, his hard cock reaching all the way to his navel. Every beautiful inch of his body called to her and she held out her arms to welcome him. He came down on top of her carefully, capturing her lips with his, their tongues rubbing and stroking until she was on fire. Flames licked through her veins and she rubbed herself against his softness, letting his masculine scent wrap around her.

This was the man she loved. She wanted to express those feelings with her body, her lips, and her fingers. She let her hands wander down his torso and wrapped her hands around his cock, moving them in a rhythm well known to them both.

"Fuck, baby. That feels so fucking good." He pulled her hands off of him with a groan. "Too good. I want this to last."

She lifted one of his fingers into her mouth, sucking and licking it, letting him know in no uncertain terms what she had in mind.

"You want to suck my cock, sweetheart? I love having your hot mouth around my dick."

Jason moved up so he was straddling her torso, his cock inches from her mouth. She piled pillows behind her head so she was in the perfect position before engulfing the purplish-red head in her mouth. She licked at the slit drawing a tortured moan and his hands closed around the back of her head, tangling in her long hair. She moved her mouth up and down, as far as she could take him, swallowing on him until he pulled from her mouth, his expression desperate.

"For the love of God, stop, sweetheart. I want to come inside you."

She smiled up at him playfully. "That would have been inside of me."

Jason reached down and pulled the pillows from behind her head and hauled her down on the mattress so she was lying flat. "In your pussy, inside you. I think you want it, too."

She did want it. He rummaged in his jean's pocket for a condom and rolled it on before coming down on top of her. The heat from his body and the feel of his skin under her palms sent her arousal soaring into the clouds. This was how it was supposed to be.

He pressed into her slowly, letting her body adjust to the invasion. When he was in to the hilt, he relaxed, taking his weight on his elbows. He took his time kissing her mouth, jaw, nose, and ears before working his way down her neck and shoulders. She was a shuddering mess by the time he pulled part way out and thrust back in, running his cock over her sweet spot. Jason knew exactly where to fuck her to drive her over the edge. He proceeded to do just that, slowly, taking his time with each stroke.

He never lost eye contact as he eased himself in and out of her trembling body. Time slowed down and she drifted in a world where there was only herself, Jason, and the wondrous sensations they created together. When her orgasm came, it washed over like waves on the shore. She gave herself up to it, crying out his name as he thrust inside her on last time. His cock seemed to swell inside her and he muttered her name with his face buried in her neck.

She held on to him for a long time and only let him go when he had to dispose of the condom. He came back, spooning her in the bed, whispering funny things he'd remembered about the past and things he wanted to do in the future. He fell asleep some time later, but Sami couldn't find the same peace.

Somehow, she had to hold on to what she'd found this second time with Gabe and Jason. The problem was she didn't know how. Gabe and Jason had said they'd take care of everything, but she couldn't expect them to do that. She'd learned she had to take care of herself. Depending on others was an iffy proposition. Even if those others were two of the most wonderful men in the entire world. Her men. She needed to figure a way out of this herself. It was her problem, not theirs.

Her past was still out to get her and she wasn't the naive girl she'd been before. She couldn't have her future with these men without putting her past behind her.

Once and for all.

Chapter Ten

Sadie was getting settled on the couch when Sami heard a rap on the front door. She and Jason had brought Sadie back here to Plenty when she was released from the hospital this morning. She seemed relieved to be leaving Orlando and although exhausted and in pain, she was smiling more than Sami could remember in recent memory.

"I got it, sweetheart." Jason headed to the front door, letting her continue tucking a blanket around Sadie's feet and handing her the remote.

"You're spoiling me," Sadie said. "I can't sit around here for long. I need to get up and get a job."

"Don't worry about that." Gabe walked into the living room and handed Sadie a glass of orange juice. "Everything is covered. Heal up and then we'll find you a job."

Gabe used what she was calling his Dom voice, and she shivered at the deep timbre. Perhaps she could convince him to use it on her when they were alone at the club sometime. And maybe they could use that X thing she'd seen people strapped to when she worked. That looked pretty hot. She'd heard subs scream when they climaxed, the pleasure was so intense.

Jason was ushering Ryan Parks into the living room and two men she'd never met before. The men shook hands with Gabe while Ryan performed the introductions.

"Sami, I'd like you to meet Logan Farraday and Meyer Smith. They recently moved to Plenty and opened an investigations firm. One of the things they do is deep background checks. We think it would be a good idea to have them run a check on this Ray

Campbell."

She looked accusingly at Gabe and he had the nerve to simply shrug. "Ryan needed to be told, Samantha. You said Ray's going to head here. We have to be ready for him."

Ryan offered his hand to Sadie. "I'm Sheriff Ryan Parks. I believe you're Sadie?"

Sami smacked her forehead. "I'm sorry I didn't introduce you both. I didn't get much sleep last night."

Sadie shook Ryan's hand, her eyes darting to Logan and Meyer. Logan seemed to recognize her unease and knelt next to her to shake hands, holding her hand gently and frowning at the bruises covering every exposed inch of Sadie's skin.

"I'm Logan Farraday. We want to help you, if we can. Did Ray Campbell do this to you, Miss Stewart?" he asked softly. Sadie swallowed and nodded, twisting the blanket between her fingers nervously. "We'll do everything in our power to catch this animal. No one should have to go through what you've gone through."

Logan's voice was soft but threaded with steel. It was clear he was livid at what had happened to Sami's friend. She felt better already, knowing he felt so passionate about this cause.

Meyer cleared his throat. "What can you tell us about this man? No detail is too small."

He'd pulled out a laptop and his fingers were poised over the keys. Sami took a deep breath. She didn't like talking about Ray in the least.

"He told me he went to Cornell, in their hospitality management program. He said his parents were dead, but he does have a brother. A half-brother. I met him once. I liked him, although it was clear there was tension between the two of them. His name is Terry Sheldon."

Meyer, his expression impassive, typed away as she spoke. Everyone was quiet while she tried to remember every little thing she could.

"He told me he was twenty-nine and had never been married. No kids. He grew up in upstate New York but had been wanting to move to Florida for a long time." She shrugged. "That's about all I really know. It sounds pathetic when I really think about it."

Logan pulled the ottoman close to the couch and sat down. "What about his likes and dislikes. Food, music, places, movies?"

"That would be helpful?" Sami asked in surprise.

Meyer nodded. "Sometimes it's the smallest things that make a difference. We once were able to find details on a woman who loved handbags. Turned out she went shopping in a particular store quite a bit. She talked to one of the clerks there, thinking no one would ever know. Logan talked to the clerk and our client was able to pinpoint how she was selling their trade secrets to the competition."

"Wow," Sadie marveled. "That's amazing. Just from purses?"

"Just from purses," Logan agreed.

"Ray liked coffee," Sami offered. "I guess I should say he loved it. He went to the Starbucks across the street from the hotel a couple of times a day, every day. He always had a cup in his hand."

Meyer's fingers tapped on the keyboard. "That's great. Anything else?"

Sami recounted everything she could remember, including the names of friends she had never met, and that he liked pepperoni on his pizza.

"This is great." Logan smiled. "I don't suppose you have a picture of Ray Campbell? It would help."

Sami shook her head but then nodded. She stood and headed for the stairs. "Hold on a second."

She went to her room and rummaged through a box retrieved from the apartment. She finally found what she was looking for in a dusty folder. She flew down the stairs and handed it to Logan.

"It's a picture they took of the five of us in the management training program. That's Ray on the end."

Meyer looked up from his laptop with a smile. "This is great. I can scan it in and enlarge it. Maybe run some facial recognition on it."

Jason whistled. "You make small town law enforcement look backward."

Meyer chuckled, snapping his laptop shut. "Let's just say I like playing with my computer."

Ryan looked from Sami to Sadie. "Here are the rules. I hope you follow them better than Cassie and Jillian did. When you go somewhere, you need to have someone with you. When you're home, leave the doors and windows locked."

Logan nodded. "Also, always have a cell phone turned on and charged. If anything happens to you, we can track you through it."

Sami's eyes went wide. "You can track us through our cell phones? I had no idea."

Logan pointed to Meyer. "He can. He can probably tell you where the President of the United States is at this very moment. I've learned to just sit back and let him do his thing. I don't want to know the details of how he does it."

Gabe laughed. "Wise man. If you guys need anything else, let us know."

Logan cleared his throat. "Thanks. Will Miss Stewart be staying here if we need to talk to her?"

Before Sami could answer, Sadie piped up. "Not for too long. As soon as I have a job, I'll be looking for a place of my own."

"No way." Jason shook his head. "You're staying here at least until Ray is caught. Besides, you need to get some rest and heal."

"I need to find a job," Sadie insisted. "I'm not a freeloader."

Sami patted Sadie's hand, still covered in bruises from where she'd tried to fight off Ray. "Of course you're not a freeloader. Jason is right. You need to heal and we need to find Ray. Until then, you're staying here."

Meyer stood up. "I don't mean to stick my nose in where it's not wanted, but what do you do, Miss Stewart? What kind of work are you looking for?"

Sadie shrugged. "I'm not picky. I was a waitress in Orlando, and

I've also done clerical work."

Logan's eye lit up. "You mean like answer phones and handle correspondence?"

"Sure, stuff like that. I put invoices into a computer and kept schedules. I'm good with numbers, too."

"Perfect. You can work with us." Logan grinned triumphantly. "We're just getting our office up and running here, and we could use some administrative help. What do you say?"

It was the first truly happy smile from Sadie, Sami had seen in a long time. "That would be great. I can start right away."

"No, you can't." Meyer shook his head. "Get well first. How about we say a week from today? That will give us time to get the office ready for a third person. We need to order a desk and another computer."

"That sounds like a good idea." Gabe jumped in before Sadie could protest. "Looks like everything is working out fine."

Sadie sat back on the pillows and smiled at Logan and Meyer. "Thank you for giving me a chance. You won't regret it. I'll work very hard."

Logan waved away her thanks. "You're helping us. We really need someone. If you'll excuse us, we need to get started on the investigation."

Sami hid a smile at the way Meyer and Logan had neatly cornered Sadie. They both had made it sound as if she'd be helping them not the other way around.

The five men headed outside and Sami turned to Sadie. "See? Everything is going to be okay. You'll get better, and start a new job. Things are looking up."

Sadie sipped at her orange juice. "What about Ray?"

"One thing at a time. Looks like Meyer and Logan are more than capable of finding something out about him that can help us get him off my back, and by extension, your back."

Sadie's gaze went to where the two men had been sitting. "They do seem like they know what they're doing. Very smart."

Sami nudged her. "And cute."

"I guess. If you like the type." Sadie wouldn't meet Sami's eyes.

"The cute and smart type. Yeah, you're right. They're the worst. Probably a couple of animals."

Sadie's lips twitched. "I know what you're trying to do, and it won't work. The last thing I need is a man. Or two. I'm still reeling from our conversation this morning when you told me about Plenty and how people like ménages here. I'm trying to wrap my mind around it but I honestly don't understand it. I'm here to get my life together. Not find love."

"Plenty is the place to do it. Just wait. In a few weeks, it'll feel like home."

* * * *

"You need to learn to defend yourselves. I know Sami can shoot, but you need to know as well, Sadie."

Jason pulled his SUV over to the side of the road, way out by the quarries. He'd set up a shooting range out here where they wouldn't bother anyone. It had been Ryan's idea to make sure the women knew how to shoot a real weapon, but Jason had wholeheartedly agreed. Waiting for some asshole to show up was not Jason's idea of fun. He really needed to talk to Ryan about doing something more proactive once they received Logan and Meyer's report on Ray Campbell.

Sadie was feeling much better in the last three days and already was talking about wanting to start her new job. She wasn't ready to work a full day, but he could get her out of the house for a few hours with a shooting lesson. The weather was perfect, sunny and mild, and already both women were looking more relaxed than they had in days.

"It's been years since I've shot a weapon. I think I was twelve." Sami chuckled, clearly delighted about today's events. "I was a pretty good shot, too."

Sadie, on the other hand, had a frown on her face. "I've never even held a real gun. I wouldn't know what to do."

Jason pulled his gun case from the back seat. "That's why we're here. You don't need to be a great shot, but you do need to learn the basics of how to handle a weapon safely. You never know when it will come in handy."

He walked them over to where he'd set up the range. Tin cans were lined up on a big log about twenty feet away. He pulled out the .22 Ruger and held it up.

"This is a 22. It's a small caliber pistol and lighter and less powerful than many of the handguns out there, and has almost no recoil. Don't be fooled. This gun can kill you or the person you're pointing it at. So, lesson number one. Don't point any weapon at anything you don't intend to shoot. Got it?"

Both women nodded, and Sami even smiled. She looked like she couldn't wait to get her hands on the pistol and fire off a few rounds. He pulled the clip from his vest pocket and held it up. "This is the clip that holds the ammunition. You take the clip and slide it in here." Jason pushed the clip into the pistol grip until it clicked. "Then you pull the slide back to chamber a round into the chamber. Now you're ready to shoot. Any questions?"

"That's it?" Sadie's brows were drawn together. "That seems too easy."

"We're lucky. The days of muskets and packing gun powder are over. Do you want to take the first shot?"

Sadie backed away with a shake of her head. "I'll let Sami take the first shot."

Sami was eager to take her turn and he handed both the women foam earplugs before standing behind her with his hands under her elbows. He could feel her take a deep breath as she took aim at the cans.

"Just line up the sights on your target and squeeze the trigger slowly."

Sami fired and none of the cans fell. "Shit."

"Relax. You haven't shot a weapon for a long time. Just relax and try again."

It took two more rounds, but she finally hit one of the cans. She jumped around like she'd won a giant stuffed animal at the fair.

"Careful, babe. We don't celebrate too much while holding a loaded weapon."

Sami giggled but calmed down. He let her fire off several rounds until she'd knocked all the cans down.

"Great job. I'll set up more cans and then it will be Sadie's turn."

Sadie gulped. "Do I have to?"

"You do," Jason nodded firmly. "It was Sheriff Ryan's idea. Logan and Meyer thought it was a good idea, as well." Jason had noticed the chemistry between Sadie and the two men. He hoped it would lead somewhere, but in the meantime, her protection was his and Gabe's responsibility. A responsibility they took seriously.

The mention of the Sheriff and her new employers seemed to get her attention. She lifted her chin and nodded. "Okay, I'll learn."

He set more cans up on the log, reloaded the clip and inserted it into the pistol, and then pressed it in her hands. She was shaking a little and he let her relax and aim as long as she needed to. Her first shot went off wildly, along with her next several. She'd emptied two clips before she finally hit one of the cans.

Sami lifted her arms in victory. "Yes! That's the way. Shoot 'em in the balls, Sadie."

Jason choked on his own spit trying not to laugh. His woman was bloodthirsty. He'd hate to be this Ray guy if he came around now. Sami wasn't the beaten down, cowed woman who had arrived in Plenty mere weeks ago. Nor was this the sweet, naive girl who'd left a few years ago. This was a woman who could clearly take care of herself. He and Gabe better watch their damn step or she'd have their hides.

Sadie seemed to be in the spirit as well. She pretended to blow on the muzzle of the gun and grinned. "I think I'm a natural at this."

Jason ran his hand through his hair. "This day is not turning out as I planned. I didn't expect you to enjoy this so much."

Sami rolled her eyes. "You think only men like shooting a gun? Chauvinist."

"I'm not a chauvinist. Can we get back to things? Sadie, why don't you go ahead and empty this clip."

She did and managed to hit two more cans. Jason eased the gun from her eager fingers, ejected the clip and slipped it back into its case. He would clean it later.

"I think that's enough for the day. You did well. I want you ladies to take this seriously. This threat is real and your need to defend yourself is real. I don't want anyone to get hurt." He looked at Sadie's fading bruises. "Or hurt again. Seriously, I mean it."

Sadie nodded. "We're taking it seriously. Aren't we, Sami?" Sadie gave Sami a warning look and Sami toned down her jubilance immediately. Looked like there was a spine of steel underneath Sadie's soft-spoken way.

"We take it seriously," Sami said. "I'm just excited, that's all."

"It's okay to be excited. It's okay to be happy. I wasn't trying to bring down the entire conversation."

"Well, in that case." Sami jumped into his arms, wrapping her arms and legs around him. "Can we go to the diner for lunch? It's pot roast day. Please? Pretty please?"

He was sure he'd gotten through to her about the seriousness of the situation, and he couldn't refuse this woman anything. He loved the pot roast at the diner just as much as she did.

"Three pot roast lunches coming right up. Do you want pie or cake to go with that?"

"Pie."

"Cake."

Both Sami and Sadie answered at the same time.

"I think we can do both. Let's get in the truck and head out. I'm starved."

As they drove away, Jason took a look into the rearview mirror. He only hoped protecting them from Ray Campbell was as easy as teaching them to shoot.

* * * *

Gabe twisted open a longneck and leaned against the kitchen counter. Brayden, Falk, and Josh had a crowd this Monday night for poker and everyone appeared to be having a good time eating, drinking, and shooting the shit. Gabe wasn't planning on staying late tonight though. He'd dropped off Sadie and Sami at the diner for their Monday night dinner and he would be picking them up as well. He didn't want them out and about by themselves until Ray Campbell was behind bars.

Logan and Meyer joined him in the kitchen, Meyer grabbing a slice of pizza and Logan opening a soda.

"Damn, the pizza in this town is out of this world," marveled Meyer. "Much better than anything we got in LA."

"LA isn't known for its pizza." Logan laughed. "Listen, we're glad we ran into you. We're still working on the background for Ray Campbell but I think we'll have the full dossier tomorrow."

Gabe's lips twisted. "How about a preview?"

Meyer shook his head. "Sorry, we need to confirm what we've found first. I don't want to tell you something then find out that it wasn't true. We deal in facts, and facts only."

Ryan came up behind Logan and slapped him on the back. "Did I hear something about facts? Do you have any information yet?"

Logan held up his hand. "Not yet. We were just telling Gabe we don't want to say anything until we know we are one hundred percent correct. Hopefully, we'll have something concrete to tell you tomorrow. We have several calls out for confirmations."

Jason joined the group, tossing a few pretzels in his mouth. "Did

Sadie help you with the investigation? Today was her first day. How did it go?"

The normally unsmiling Meyer's face lit up. "She did great. We didn't have her do anything with this investigation but we have her going through files and organizing things. She's going to do a good job for us. I'm glad we hired her."

Zach and Chase Harper sidled up and helped themselves to pizza and a beer. "What did we miss? We just got here."

Ryan laughed. "Fatherhood putting a crimp in your schedule? You do look a little tired."

Cassie Harper, Zach and Chase's wife had just delivered a baby girl two months ago. They were over the moon with happiness but still adjusting to having a tiny tyrant keeping them up at night and basically running the household. Zach bit into the pizza with relish. "I love our little angel but it would be awesome if she slept through the night. Poor Cassie is more tired than we are. We offered to give Sabrina bottles at night, but Cassie is determined to breast feed."

Mark and Travis had been hovering around the perimeter of the group but perked up at the mention of baby Sabrina. "Has Cassie tried pumping? That's what Becca did so we could feed Noah at night." Travis started filling his plate with wings and chips.

Chase shook his head. "She hasn't had any luck pumping."

Jack Parks rolled his eyes and grimaced. "Listen to us. We're men, for fuck's sake. We should be talking about sports and boobs, not babies."

Travis grinned. "Technically, I was talking about boobs."

"All I'm say, is we're one step away from handing in our man card. Next thing you know we'll be comparing notes on how to be more understanding when the woman are PMSing. Shit. Now that Jillian's pregnant, I'm not getting all sensitive," Jack declared.

Ryan pointed to Jack. "Yes, you will. You go all gooey when you see Jillian. Don't even pretend you're Charles Bronson. You're more like Mr. Rogers."

Jack blushed as the men laughed and ribbed him some more. It was all good-natured as Gabe knew every man here was head over heels for their woman. Even Logan and Meyer looked smitten with Sadie, although it was early days yet.

Mark opened a fresh beer. "I find getting Becca a nice glass of wine really helps her cramps and mood swings."

Jack groaned and the men laughed some more. Jason finally stepped into the middle of the group to get their attention. "Listen, I do have something to bring up. This waiting around for Ray Campbell to show up is starting to wear on me. I think it's wearing on the women as well. If we learned anything from when Danny Trent came to town is that we need to be on the offensive, not the defensive."

Chase rubbed his shoulder where Trent had shot him. "I'll agree with that. What did you have in mind and how can we help?"

"Maybe we could set some sort of a trap. Lure him here and then catch him before he has a chance to hurt anyone."

Ryan rubbed his chin. "It could work. I agree, sitting around and waiting isn't the best idea. What were you thinking we'd lure him with?"

Jason nodded toward Logan and Meyer. "Right now, I'd say money would be a good lure, but perhaps these guys will have something even better from their investigation."

Logan leaned forward on the counter, propped on his elbows. "No matter what we find, money is a powerful motivator for any criminal."

"When you get your investigation done, we should all meet again and discuss a plan," Ryan said. "I like the idea of having more control this time. It should never have gone the way it did with Trent."

Gabe tossed his beer into the trash with satisfaction. He was glad to hear everyone was on the same page as far as being proactive in going after this guy. It felt better to take action than to sit around and wait. He'd learned a hell of a lot of patience in the last few years, but this was stretching him thin. He wanted Ray Campbell out of their lives.

* * * *

Sami marveled at the group of women gathered for Monday Night Dinner at the Diner. She'd brought Sadie with her, and on her other side was Lacey. Across the table was Ava, Becca, Leah, and Cassie with Jillian on Sadie's other side. Baby Noah was ensconced at the end of the table right next to Becca holding court. He was currently eating a soggy dinner roll and waving to everyone that came in the entrance.

Cassie held a sleeping baby Sabrina in the crook of her left arm while she tried to eat her dinner with her right hand. They'd all offered to hold the cute-as-a-button two-month-old, but Cassie shook her head and said she was used to it. Sabrina was very much a mommy's girl and liked to be held by her, otherwise she was fussy.

"What do you think the men are talking about tonight?" Cassie signaled to the waitress for more iced tea.

Jillian giggled. "The usual, sports, boobs, sex, dirt, beer. Maybe trucks, too."

"They think we're talking about the wedding, but I'm sick of talking about the wedding." Ava sighed.

Becca patted her hand. "You're getting married this weekend, thank goodness. Then you can talk about being pregnant."

Ava shook her head in denial. "I already told the boys I'm not getting knocked up for at least six months, maybe longer. Look at Jillian, she held out for a while."

Jillian sipped her water. "We wanted to wait until Ryan had his hours under control. Then it took a few months to get pregnant. It's not like they tell you in high school. Getting pregnant, even with two men, wasn't easy. It seemed like every time I was fertile, both men were on duty."

Sami played with her glass until finally Leah's gaze zeroed in on her. "You've been very quiet, Sami. Want to tell us what's on your mind?"

"Maybe." Sami chewed her lip. She and Sadie had been talking a lot about Ray Campbell. "The thing is, Sadie and I have been talking about how it sucks just sitting here waiting for Ray to show up and be an asshole."

Cassie nodded. "I think Jillian and I will say an 'amen' to that. We were stuck inside a house for days. At least you two get to come into town as long as you're not alone."

"It still sucks." Sami rolled her eyes. "I don't like having a babysitter. When I came back to town, it was on new terms with the men. I'm a grown woman, not a naive little girl anymore. I want to be treated like a woman who can handle her own problems. I don't want Jason and Gabe to have to handle this for me. I got myself into this mess, I need to get myself out."

Lacey, who had been quiet most of the evening, leaned in with a smile. "So, what's the plan?"

"I don't really have a plan. Yet." Sami shook her head. "Okay, maybe I do. I was thinking I could call him and tell him I have some more money for him and lure him to Plenty. Then I was thinking I might be able to scare him. Everyone says he doesn't have anything to hold over my head since I didn't know what the packages I was holding at the front desk for him contained."

"You have his phone number?" Ava gasped. "Has he called you?"

"He doesn't have my new number." Sami held up her phone. "I have his number unless he's changed it. If it's the same, I can call him anytime."

The women all exchanged looks, silently debating the plan. Finally, Becca spoke up. "I like the idea of luring him here. You could lure him to Original Sin. Once he's there, well, there are many things at the club that would scare the shit out of a man."

"I doubt he'd be afraid of me," Sami said.

Ava frowned. "How big is he?"

Sami shrugged. "Average height and build. Maybe he's five nine or five ten, slim. Not a body builder but not a weakling either."

Jillian tapped her nail on the table. "We can take him. If we all help, he won't stand a chance."

Sami held up her hand. "I can't ask you to take that kind of a chance."

Sadie placed her hand on Sami's arm. "I want to. I'm in. I owe this asshole some grief."

The other women nodded. "We know you need to do this to prove to the men you can handle things yourself. But there's nothing wrong with a little help from your friends, is there?" Becca's eyes lit up with mischief. "I haven't kicked any butt since Cassie's bachelorette party."

Every woman at the table had a huge grin and sparkly eyes. "I don't want to get you in trouble with your men." Sami wanted to make sure they knew what they were getting into. It might be dangerous. Ray was a bully with absolutely no remorse of any kind.

Ava slapped the table with a laugh. "Honey, that's the best part. You're fixing to get in trouble with your men. Why shouldn't we?"

When they put it that way, Sami couldn't argue. She smiled, feeling like things just might turn out okay after all.

"If you think you might want to do this, here's the plan I've been pondering. Any ideas you have, I want to hear them."

Chapter Eleven

"I'm not sure about this," Gary protested. "What if Gabe gets mad and fires me?"

It was Tuesday afternoon and the women were gathered at Original Sin to practice the plan to scare Ray into leaving Sami alone. All they needed was Gary's cooperation but it was looking dicey. They'd managed to get him here even though it was his day off, but he had a very dubious expression on his face when they told him he needed to let them tie him up.

"He won't fire you, I promise. I'm just playing a little joke on him. He has a great sense of humor. He'll love it."

Gary's brows were knitted together. He was a very reluctant volunteer. Lacey patted him on the back and started leading him to the back room. "It's easy. All you have to do is let us practice tying you up. We want you to struggle a little bit, but not the first time. This will be quick. We promise."

"Is this like the time you let all the frogs go in biology when we were in high school?"

Sami had forgotten Gary went to high school with them. He'd been in a different crowd but apparently word had gotten around about her and Lacey's stunt.

"It was inhumane what they were doing to those frogs," Lacey said firmly. "We did what we had to do."

They positioned Gary in the middle of the back room and the women circled him. Since Jillian was pregnant, they'd made her the director of their little play and she was in full General mode. She pointed to Gary.

"Now you start to move toward Sami and we'll try and stop you. Don't struggle too hard this first time. We're learning the ropes so to speak in this round."

Gary lumbered forward and the women surrounded him, pushing him toward the spanking bench and trying to attach him to it. After much huffing and puffing, Jillian called them all together.

"The spanking bench isn't working. Even when he's not really trying, he's too strong to bend over like that. We might have better luck with the St. Andrew's cross. Also, we need to disorient him. If he can't see clearly, we'll have the advantage."

Sami walked over and flipped a few switches, turning off the bright overhead lights used during the day and turning on the smaller spotlights used when the backroom was in play mode. There were plenty of dark spaces and shadows to get lost in and frustrate a visitor who didn't know the club well.

"Better?"

Jillian nodded. "Much better."

"How about this?" Becca held up a large piece of black fabric. "It will fit right over his head."

"You're not putting that on me." Gary pointed. "I won't do it."

Gary had been a good sport so far, but he was digging his heels in now and Sami couldn't let him. She hated to do it, but she was going to have to beg a little.

"Please, Gary. We really need to practice this. It's so important to me." She leaned in so only he could hear her. "I'm trying to show him I'm ready to submit to him. Please." She looked up at him with her best pleading eyes and his expression softened.

"Man, is that what you're doing? This seems a weird way to go about it, but hell yes, I'll help you. Let's do this."

Sami felt a tiny bit guilty lying to a really nice guy like Gary but she sure as hell couldn't tell him the truth. Men stuck together and he would certainly tell Jason and Gabe. Then they'd try and take care of this for her. She couldn't let that happen.

After several run-throughs, Gary was seriously fighting back and the women were able to wrestle him to the St. Andrew's cross and get him hooked to it without much fuss. Jillian declared their rehearsal a success. Gary looked exhausted and eager to leave.

"Can I go now? I won't tell Gabe, I promise."

As soon as Sami nodded, Gary was headed to the door. "Thank you!" she called after him. The other women were breaking open water bottles. It had been a real workout.

"Ray's going to fight back harder. I think Gary was afraid to really let loose on us," Sami warned.

"We're ready for him." Sadie rubbed her hands together. "We know what we need to do and how to do it. The black bag over the head was a genius idea. It totally disoriented him."

"You're welcome," Becca grinned. "I read too many spy novels obviously."

Lacey nudged Sami. "Go ahead. Call him."

She took a deep breath and grabbed her phone, punching in a few buttons. She put it on speaker so the other women could hear as it rang. She was about to hang up when Ray answered.

"Ray."

Sami swallowed hard. She'd underestimated how difficult it would be to talk to him. "Ray? It's Sami James."

"Sami, it's about time I heard from you. I guess you got the message I left you at your apartment."

Sadie had a pissed off expression and her middle finger high in the air, pointed directly at the phone. Sami had to concentrate to keep a straight face.

"I did. Listen, I have some money for you."

"You better." Ray's voice was cold. "It better be a lot of money. I've been waiting for you. I don't want to have to go send another message through your friend."

"I came into some money. That's why I left Orlando. You can have it all if you'll leave me alone once and for all."

There was a pause and she thought he wasn't going to go for the bait. "How much? It better be five figures or you're wasting my time."

Relief flooded her body and she grinned at the women listening intently.

"It is. Fifty thousand. All you have to do is come get it."

"I'll be there tonight. Where are you?"

Ava waved silently in the air and Sami nodded. "I don't have it yet." Ray swore but she continued as if she hadn't heard him. "I'll have it by the end of the week. You can meet me on Friday night around eight o'clock. I'll give you the address."

"Fine. Let me get a pen."

Sami recited the address and directions to Original Sin. "Come to the back door behind the building. I'll let you in."

"I want cash, Sami. Don't try and pawn off a rubber check on me."

The women were grinning and pumping their fists in the air. "Don't worry, it'll be cash. I just want this over with. Once I give you the money, you'll leave me alone, right?"

Sami tried to put as much naiveté into her words as possible and Ray seemed fooled. "Of course, Sami. You'll never see me again."

Ray hung up and Sami high-fived Sadie. "We did it!"

Sadie hugged Sami. "Now we only have to wait."

Sami shook her head, grinning evilly. "Actually, we have something else to do." She picked up a heavy flogger from a table. "We need to practice with some of this stuff. We're not going to actually hurt him, but I want Ray so scared he's peeing his pants. I want him to leave me alone from now on."

Cassie eyed the implements on the walls and tables. "We put him on the cross and swish these things around, telling him you know the truth, that should do it."

"I hope so. I'm done with Ray Campbell. On Friday, I'm taking my life back."

* * * *

Sami pushed a plastic tombstone into the soft earth in the front yard, stepped back, and smiled. The yard was coming together and already it had a spooky, scary air. When Jason and Gabe had told her the entire street in their neighborhood decorated their houses and lawns for Halloween, Sami had been excited. Halloween was a popular holiday in Plenty to begin with, but this was icing on the cake.

It was Tuesday evening and dusk was starting to settle over them, but the neighborhood was lively as everyone seemed to be out tonight setting up graveyards, flying ghosts, and screeching witches.

"We need more cobwebs to hang from the trees. I want this to look awesome so we can send pictures to Gran. She's already bugging me for them. Apparently, they decorate at the rehabilitation center, too. She wants me to bring her more plastic spiders on my next visit." Sami pointed to the two large oak trees in the front yard. Gabe grimaced but obediently began to climb the ladder to string the intricate webbing from the higher branches. Jason pulled into the drive, smiling as he took in the activities of the street.

"Deputy Jason reporting for duty." Jason gave her a mock salute and clicked his heels together. "I'm guessing I'm not even going to get a beer before you put me to work."

"You can get a beer and change. Gabe's doing a great job, but he'll need help stretching those cobwebs."

Jason looked up at Gabe perched on the ladder. "We have cobwebs? I thought we had a couple of tombstones and an old ghost."

Gabe laughed almost pitching himself off the ladder. "I gave her a decoration budget and she and Sadie outdid themselves. We'll be out here until midnight putting all this stuff up."

"Some of it's for the inside of the house." Sadie laughed as she unboxed a strand of skull lights. "We'll have the best haunted house on the street."

"I want to win," Sami said. "The homeowner's association is having a contest and with all this stuff we should win first place."

Jason scratched his head. "What do we win?"

"I don't know. Bragging rights?" Sami shrugged. Wasn't winning enough? She didn't need a prize.

"Hey, neighbors." Logan and Meyer were walking up the sidewalk. "Plenty sure takes its Halloween seriously. We've never seen anything like it." Logan looked around at the decorations. "This is amazing. Some of this is worthy of being in a haunted house or maybe even a movie."

Meyer stepped closer to the tombstone reading the funny limerick written on it. "Here lies my nagging wife. Now she's dead and I'm loving life."

The corners of Meyer's lips tilted up. "Poor woman was probably miserable."

"Most men are more trouble than they're worth." Sadie started wrapping the strand of lights in the bushes.

"I don't know about that." Meyer came up beside her and started to help her. "Some men are worth it." He gave Logan a meaningful glance. Sadie's face turned bright pink.

"A few, I guess. What brings you gentleman here tonight?"

Logan laughed softly and pitched in on Sadie's other side, effectively closing her in so if she moved either to her right or left, she'd run into one of the men. "Are you tired of us already? You've only been working for us for two days."

Sadie looked speechless but Logan seemed to take pity on her. "Actually we came to tell you what we found in our investigation. It's quite interesting. Fascinating, really."

He had everyone's attention. They all stopped what they were doing, and Gabe descended the ladder to put his arm around Sami's shoulders. She leaned against his strength as her heart rate accelerated. She'd already called Ray to make arrangements to see him. She hoped she wouldn't hear anything tonight that would make her second guess her decision.

Logan took the lead. "Ray Campbell is only one of his names. We found his real identity. His real name is Ray Harold. We found out quite by accident. I went to talk to some people that might know him and visited a coffee shop near the hotel you used to work at. She remembers him coming in every day. One day he paid by credit card. The name on the credit card was Bill Gardner. The reason she remembered is that the name was different than what he'd told her his name was. She asked him about it, worried about a stolen credit card and he made up some excuse about using a different name because he had an old girlfriend who wouldn't leave him alone."

Gabe frowned. "How did that help you find out his name was Ray Harold?"

"When I ran Bill Gardner," Meyer answered, "you wouldn't believe what came up. Wants, warrants. This guy has a bunko sheet a mile long."

Jason shook his head. "You must have it wrong. He deals drugs. It should be a vice record."

Logan grinned. "No, it's bunko. Ray Campbell Harold Gardner is a con artist and wanted in about ten states." He turned to Sami. "You never held on to his drugs. You didn't do a damn thing illegally. He only made you think you had so he could extort money from you."

Sami sagged against Gabe for support. She wanted to believe him, but... "But Marion said it was drugs and Ray didn't even argue with her. He acted like it was true. It had to be drugs."

Meyer nodded. "Ah yes, Marion. She was in on it, Sami. Marion is actually Sandra Harold. She's Ray's sister. They play this con in hotel after hotel, snagging some young naive girl and making her think she's done something wrong. They also run other cons on old people and people with poor credit. Basically, anyone who is desperate or trusting. They're real pieces of work, those two. Their parents were grifters themselves. They come from a long line of this.

They learned at their parents' knee. That's why it comes so naturally and smoothly. It's simply the family business."

"And I was the most trusting of all," Sami said dryly. "God, I am so fucking stupid. I bought it hook, line, and sinker. No questions asked."

Logan put his hand on her shoulder, his expression one of sympathy. "If it makes you feel any better, Ray was running this con with about two dozen people at any given time. That's a lot of trusting people. He's a professional at this with no remorse. He made it look real."

Gabe pulled her into his arms. "You didn't do anything wrong so you're completely free of this guy. If he shows up here, we'll call Ryan and throw him in jail."

"He'll probably spend the rest of his life behind bars." Meyer handed a thick file to Sami. "Here are all the details. You'll see he spends money as fast as he gets it. He has a gambling problem but terrible luck. He couldn't pick a winner in a one horse race."

Sami didn't need to read through the details. She caught Sadie's eye and shook her head. They weren't going to say anything to the men. The only thing that had really changed was how it would all end. Sami had assumed she'd be kicking Ray out of Plenty. Now, she would be handing him over to Sheriff Ryan. But not until she told Ray she knew everything about him and what he'd done. He'd messed with the last innocent young girl.

This innocent young girl was going to give him a run for his money.

Chapter Twelve

Sami crossed and uncrossed her legs as she checked the clock on the wall for the hundredth time. The rehearsal dinner was in full swing in the bar area of Original Sin and the clock was slowing ticking toward the time when Ray would arrive. All week she'd been worried he would show up early but it appeared this one time, he was doing as she asked. Her stomach tumbled as she thought about what she'd planned to do and what she needed to do.

She motioned to Jillian across the room to join her.

Jillian sat next to her and leaned forward so no one would overhear. "I have a message from Leah. She came down with the flu so she didn't make it tonight. Is this going to mess everything up?"

Sami shook her head. "Change of plans. I'm going to talk to him alone. The idea was crazy and it doesn't prove that I'm not scared of him anymore. Only one thing will do that."

Jillian played with the charm bracelet wrapped around her left wrist. "I don't mind telling you I'm nervous hearing you say this. My husband is the sheriff, and I'm not sure I feel comfortable sending you in there by yourself."

"I'll tell him that I had to do this myself. I have to stand up to Ray. Finally. He's been running my life too long."

Ava rushed toward them, looking nervously over her shoulder. "Shit, my men are following me around all night. I can't get one minute on my own. I'm afraid I won't be able to duck them at the right time."

"The plans have changed. We don't get to have any fun tonight," Jillian smiled. "Sami feels she has to do this on her own."

Ava looked shocked. "You can't be alone with him. What if he comes armed or something?"

Sami chewed on her lower lip. "He won't. I've always been so terrified of him he never needed a weapon. I was a complete pushover. I won't be tonight."

Ava squared her chin. "How can we help?"

"Give me ten minutes alone with him then send in Ryan. I just need him to know I'm not his bitch any longer. I just need to stand up to him. Then Ryan can take him away."

"You all look very serious over here," Becca joined the group with a giggle.

Jillian nodded to Sami. "The plan is off. She's going in by herself."

"The hell you are. What if he tries to hurt you?" Becca asked.

"I'll knee him in the balls or grab a flogger and whip him with it." Sami tried to smile and joke.

"Maybe you should carry a flogger just in case? Hide it behind your back," Ava suggested.

"Don't worry about me. A dozen or more huge, burly men will be just on the other side of the door. I'll be fine. I have to do this. For me and for Sadie."

Ava peered over Becca's shoulder. "What's going on over there?" She nodded toward Sadie, looking flustered, flanked by Logan and Meyer. "Is something going on over there? Should we be matchmaking?"

"I don't think we need to," Becca said. "Logan and Meyer seem to be doing just fine on their own. I told them if they moved here they'd find the perfect woman. I just didn't realize Sami had to bring her to Plenty."

"Sadie's not looking for a man right now. She's been through a lot in her life."

Jillian laughed. "When you're not looking is usually when they find you. Besides, they seem like really good guys. I bet they'll treat her right."

Brayden came up behind Ava and put his arm around her shoulders with a big grin. "Who'll treat who right?"

Ava nodded toward Sadie, Logan, and Meyer. "We think they make a nice trio."

He pursed his lips in thought. "Sadie doesn't look like she's too sure about it."

Becca smiled. "We'll see about that. They work together on a daily basis. It will either end up love or hate."

Sami glanced again at the clock on the wall. It was time. "Excuse me, but I think I need to visit the ladies room." She set her drink on a table and stood up.

Becca, Ava, and Jillian all stood up as well. "I think I will, too," Ava said casually, not making eye contact with Brayden. "I need to freshen up my lipstick."

"Me, too," Becca and Jillian parroted. Sami turned so no one could see her eye roll. By the time they got to the hallway where the restrooms were located, Sami was sweating in her brand new dress. She peered over her shoulder, but no one seemed to following them.

"That was smooth," Jillian said sarcastically. "We should have just held up a sign that said, 'Look, we're up to something we don't want you to know about.'"

Sami rubbed the back of her neck. "It can't be helped now. Luckily, the men don't seem any wiser to what's going on. I need to get into position. Does anyone know where Cassie and Lacey are?"

Jillian pointed to the door to the playroom. "Don't worry about the others. I'll wrangle them. You take your place. This will be fine. I can feel it in my bones."

Sami wished she could say the same. A knot of dread had formed in her stomach and her legs felt like lead as she adjusted the lights in the playroom and took her position in front of a table of toys. This could be a disaster in the making and Jason and Gabe would be livid, not to mention Ryan.

She straightened her shoulders and lifted her chin. There was no time for second guessing her plan. She needed to be confident and determined. She needed to face Ray and this would be her only chance. If she didn't do this, there would be something missing from her life. She needed this closure to move on. Gabe and Jason would have to understand. Understanding this was understanding her.

Cassie cracked open the back door. "We hear a car coming up the drive and some lights. It's time."

Sami licked her dry lips and rubbed her clammy hands on her dress. She was a freakin' mess and Ray hadn't even arrived yet.

"Okay. Send him in and then get back into the bar."

It felt like forever but was probably only a few minutes when the back door opened and Ray entered the playroom.

It had only been a few weeks since she'd last seen him, but she was looking at him through new eyes. What had once seemed menacing now seemed weak. His jaws were becoming saggy and a paunch was starting to build around his middle these last two years. Life had made him soft, while it had made her strong.

He wasn't expecting her to be different and surprise would be on her side tonight. His expression was smug and she couldn't wait to change it to one of dismay. He wasn't going to fuck with anyone again. She'd have her say and then turn him over to Ryan in the next room.

She schooled her features to express only fear. He'd expect her to be cowed by his bluster and she didn't want to tip him off too early. She needed him arrogant and complacent. In fact, she was counting on it.

He walked into the room and stopped a few feet from her, looking around. "Interesting meeting place, Sami. I never pegged you as a freak, but then I guess we didn't date long enough for me to find out how you liked it. Too bad. We might have had some fun."

She shuddered at the thought of their few dates and her naiveté. She shrugged her shoulders. "I work here. You didn't leave me many options."

He stepped closer to the St. Andrew's cross, running his hand over the gleaming wood Gabe had so lovingly handcrafted. "Your problems are not my problems, Sami. I've told you that over and over. Now, as fun as this little reunion is, I don't want to spend my Friday night in some pissant, backwater town. Where's my money?"

His belligerent tone almost made her lose her temper but she swallowed the emotion. She needed to stay in control. Everything was riding on her shoulders.

She toed the leather bag at her feet. "It's right here." He started to move forward but she held her hand up. "First, I need you to promise me you'll leave me alone from now on. I won't hear from you ever again."

He gave her a smarmy smile that turned her stomach. How could she have ever thought he was a nice man? "Of course, I promise. Consider your debt paid in full. The police will never know what you did."

He was a fucking liar.

"You mean what you did."

He laughed, his thin lips pulled into a snarl. "Sami, Sami, it's your word against mine. I have proof. Witnesses who saw you holding those packages. What do you have?" He scoffed. "Nothing. Now give me my money so I can get out of here."

Sami nodded. "Yes, I owe you. You should get what's coming to you." She let her gaze rake over him as insolently as he'd looked at her so many times. "I know your secrets, Ray."

His smile never faltered. "Secrets? I don't have any secrets. You don't know shit."

"I know you real name is Raymond Harold."

That got his attention. For the first time since she'd known him, he didn't look completely in control. His smile was a little less confident.

"So? Lots of people have an alias."

"I know Marion is your sister."

That wiped the smile from his face. His eyes narrowed and his nostrils flared. He wasn't happy.

Too bad.

"Once again, so what? Now give me my money so I can get on the road."

She shook her head and casually reached behind her, feeling for the handle of the cane perched on the table she was leaning on. It felt solid in her hands and it calmed her down to know she wasn't defenseless should his anger flare.

"I know I didn't hold drugs. I know it was all a con."

His hands balled into fists and his face and neck went red. "You stupid, fucking cunt. You think you can threaten me? I'll see you in hell first."

Sami tilted her head, taking in this man that had dominated her life for the last two years. This moment wasn't nearly as satisfying as she'd imagined. He simply looked like a loser. A pathetic loser who hadn't deserved all the attention and worry she'd given him the last few years. She wasn't sure he deserved any more of her time, but she was in this deep now. She had to see it through. He started walking toward her.

"Stop right there."

He abruptly stopped, looking at her as if he was seeing her for the first time.

"I know you're a con artist wanted in several states." Sami smiled. "I'm your worst nightmare, Ray. I'm someone who's not afraid of you. I'm someone who sees what you really are."

His expression turned from anger to confusion. She wasn't reacting as he'd expected. He thought she'd be the same scared little Sami.

Good.

* * * *

Gabe looked around the bar and frowned. One minute Sami had been talking to Ava and Jillian and the next she was gone. He nudged Jason who was deep in conversation with Ryan.

"Did you see where Sami disappeared to?"

Jason shook his head. "She was talking to Jillian last I saw her."

"They're probably in the ladies room," Ryan suggested. "Wait, there's Jillian." He beckoned to his wife and she gave him a warm smile and made her excuses to Ambrose Winters, the head of the school board. Gabe had to admit he was envious. Ryan had it all. A beautiful wife and now a baby on the way. He wanted that for himself. He hoped they could talk Sami into it very soon. He wasn't getting any younger and damn if his biological clock wasn't ticking.

Ryan dropped a light kiss on Jillian's lips. "Sweetheart, have you seen Sami? Gabe and Jason are looking for her."

Jillian pressed her lips together and color flooded her fair skin. She turned her wrist so she could see her watch and then nodded. "I do know where she is. She wanted ten minutes, and I think it has been enough time."

Jason's eyebrows drew together. "Enough time for what?"

Jillian didn't have a chance to answer as Gary came up behind him with a strange look on his face.

"What are you doing here?" Gary pointed to him.

Gabe gave a sideways look to Jason. Perhaps Gary had been drinking on the job.

"I own the joint, Gary."

Gary shook his head. "I saw Sami heading to the playroom. She said she was playing a practical joke on you tonight. That's what all the women said. If you're here, who is she in the backroom with?"

Three heads swiveled to Jillian and she gulped as her husband gave her a stare that would have quelled a lesser human being. Instead, Jillian's eyes sparkled with defiance. Ryan had his hands full with this one.

"I was just trying to tell you when we were interrupted. Sami called Ray Campbell to Plenty with the false promise of money so she could finally stand up to him before turning him over to the police. They're in the backroom right now." Jillian's words came out in a rush.

At first the words didn't quite register. He'd thought she'd said Sami was in the playroom with Ray Campbell. When her meaning penetrated his thick skull, he found himself flying toward the door to the backroom, Jason and Ryan right on his heels. He pushed open the door and stopped dead in his tracks. His woman was holding a cane behind her back, but was outwardly calm.

So this is Ray Campbell.

Part of Gabe wanted to stomp over there and pound the little weasel into the ground. It wouldn't be difficult. He looked weak and out of shape. Ryan was trying to get around Gabe, but he grabbed Ryan's arm and shook his head with a finger to his lips. He looked at Jason for confirmation and saw his feelings reflected there. They both knew what had to be done.

Today was graduation day for Samantha. For once, they needed to trust her and let her stand up to this man who had made her life a living hell for so long. It would be easy to rush in, put a major hurt on this guy, and fix everything for her.

That was what *they wanted* to do.

It wasn't what *Samantha needed* them to do.

She needed them to stand by in case something went wrong, but otherwise, let her handle this. It wasn't the moment to be selfish and think only of themselves. If they really loved and understood her, they would put her needs first.

Ryan scowled but didn't make any more moves toward Ray and Sami. Next to Gabe, Jason appeared to be holding his breath and Gabe wasn't in much better shape. It wasn't easy to stand back, but he knew it was the right thing to do. He could hear their voices. Ray's getting angrier and Samantha's calm and strong. He felt a rush of pride at her demeanor. She'd become a formidable woman. A woman he was proud of.

"You don't know what you're saying." Ray's voice was starting to sound desperate.

"I know exactly what I'm saying. I'm not afraid of you, Ray. I can't believe I ever was. You really have a talent for making a girl feel like she's nothing. You did it to me. If I hadn't come here to Plenty to visit my grandmother, there's no telling how long I would have let you treat me this way. It stops today. You're lucky I'm not doing anything worse after what you did to Sadie."

"She was asking for it." A little spit dribbled from Ray's twisted lips. If he'd been considered handsome at some point, and Gabe doubted it, no one would think it now. He looked like a child who had a toy taken away and was about to throw a tantrum or bite another child.

Sami stepped forward and the small movement seemed to intimidate Ray. He stepped back and almost stumbled in his haste.

"So if I beat on you a little bit it would mean you were asking for it? That's what I'd tell the Sheriff anyway. He and I went to school together. He'd believe me. After all… it would only be your word against mine."

Ray held his hands up in front of him. "Now wait a minute. You can't go around beating on people. You're not the type, Sami."

There was fear in his voice. It quivered and shot up an octave. Sami still held the cane behind her back. "True. I guess you're in luck tonight. I'll let the Plenty police force deal with you. I'm guessing there are several places that want a piece of you. I'll sleep peacefully knowing you'll spend many quality years behind bars."

The mention of prison seemed to pull Ray out of his fear induced stupor. He started to back toward the door quickly intent on making his escape. Gabe, Jason, and Ryan all started to make a run for him as he pushed open the door and fled into the parking lot.

They found him easily as he tried to start a late model Sedan with no luck. When he saw then advancing, he decided to make a run for it, heading into the deserted field behind the club. It took mere moments before they overtook him easily. He was gasping, out of breath, and red faced. Hopefully, he would get some regular exercise in prison. He was woefully out of shape.

Gabe heard footsteps behind him and wasn't surprised in the least to see Logan and Meyer. He knew they had a vested interest in seeing this guy in jail. Meyer, the usually stoic one of the two, pointed to Ray Campbell.

"Is this the guy that beat up Sadie?"

Gabe nodded and had to hide his smile when Meyer's fist landed in Ray's soft gut. The man went to his knees with a groan, his breath knocked from his body. Ryan looked grim, but Meyer just waved him off. "You couldn't do it. It would have been police brutality. Arrest me if you want to, it was totally worth it."

Ryan muttered under his breath and grabbed Ray by the arm, dragging the man back into the building.

"I don't suppose you have a pair of handcuffs in this place, do you?"

Gabe laughed. "Padded, metal, or leather?"

"Metal will be fine. Deputy Jason, take control of this prisoner."

Jason grabbed Ray and put his hands behind his back, cuffing him with the set Gabe tossed him. At this point, there was a crowd in the playroom and Samantha was staring at them with her mouth open.

Jason wagged a finger at her. "We'll discuss this when we get this guy behind bars."

She nodded and then a smile bloomed on her beautiful face. "How long were you standing back there?"

Gabe and Jason exchanged glances. Jason chuckled as he pressed the prisoner's torso down on a table to subdue him. "Long enough. We heard you stand up to him. We're proud of you, sunshine."

Her eyes were shining with love. Love for them.

"You really let me handle it? Really?"

Gabe lifted her chin with his finger and looked into the deepest blue eyes he'd ever been privileged to see. "Why not? You're a grown woman, perfectly capable of handling things."

"I certainly am. I'm glad you realize it."

"This is all very romantic. When is someone going to tell me what happened here tonight?" Ryan all but growled the last few words. Jillian patted him on the back.

"Easy, babe. We can explain it all."

Ryan quirked an eyebrow. "Try me."

"Well," Jillian began, "it all started when we were having dinner at the diner on Monday night. We started to think and well, we decided this whole thing needed to be brought to an end."

"Did it ever occur to you to talk to your husband about it?" countered Ryan.

Jillian tapped her chin. "It did, but we decided against it."

Ryan slapped his forehead. "You're going to put me in an early grave, woman. Why the hell not?"

Gabe smiled and pulled Sami into his arms, Jason handed off Ray to Logan and Meyer and joined Gabe and Samantha, cuddling up to her back. "Because she needed to do this on her own."

Samantha had crossed a milestone tonight and things were going to be different. Better. Their relationship would always have its ups and downs. They were three strong people, after all.

Jason pressed a kiss to Samantha's cheek. "Maybe we should all sit down and talk through this."

Ava giggled and leaned against Falk. "Hasn't this been the best rehearsal dinner ever?" She held up a handful of wires.

Brayden brandished a flogger he'd picked up from a table. "What do you have in your hand, precious?"

Ava looked up at him with an innocent expression. "Wires from Ray Campbell's car. We didn't know which wires or hoses to pull, so we pulled everything we could."

Josh shook his head and smiled. "Remind me not to piss you off.

I'm very fond of my truck."

Travis led the way back into the bar. "I'm glad we got a sitter for tonight. I'd have hated to miss this."

Mark tapped Becca on the nose. "Don't play innocent with us. You've known what was going on. We're going to have a long talk about this when we get home."

Becca looked delighted. "Oooh, I love it when we have a long talk." She held up a long rubber hose, her fingers streaked with grease. "I even got a little party favor tonight. What part of the car is this?"

Ryan sighed and looked at his smiling wife. "I'm afraid to ask what you ripped from his car."

Jillian pulled her hands from behind her back, her car part dangling from her fingers. Jack burst into laughter.

"Honey, that's an air filter. A car can be driven without an air filter. It wouldn't have stopped him from getting away."

Jillian tossed the filter into a trash can and reached for a bar towel to wipe the grease from her hands. "As Ava said, we just grabbed everything that we could so he couldn't drive away. You're welcome, Ryan."

"Thank you, baby. It was actually pretty brilliant of you ladies to think about his car. We might have had another car chase on our hands."

Zach held up two fingers, ordering a couple more beers. "Considering how the last one turned out, thank goodness we didn't. It's time we face it. These women have us chasing our tails."

"You admit it, bro." Chase laughed. "I'll never admit it."

Cassie stood watching them, her eyes narrowed and her toe tapping on the floor. Chase gulped. "Shit."

"You'll be sleeping on the pool table, Chase Harper, with that attitude."

"Aw, babe. I don't know what I'm saying these days. I'm sleep deprived because of the baby."

Cassie stalked off and Chase followed her to plead his case. Gabe fell back in a chair as two on duty deputies marched Ray Campbell to a cruiser and drove off. Jason slumped in an adjacent chair.

"All this so our woman could stand up to her past. Therapy might have been easier."

Jason was yanking his chain. Gabe took the bait anyway. "Trust me, therapy is messy and painful. This was easier, believe it or not. Besides, this wasn't only about her. It was about us trusting her. We had to prove it."

Samantha knelt between them, holding their hands. "You did prove it. I love you."

Gabe stroked his chin. "How much?"

Her eyes danced and her smile grew. "Bunches and bunches."

"Care to prove it when everyone leaves? There's an entire room of toys back there to be explored. A mature woman is ready for things like that."

She squeezed their hands and nodded. "It's a date. Now get everyone out of here."

Gabe checked his watch. If he played his cards right, he could have everyone out by ten.

He couldn't wait to introduce Samantha to his dungeon. One look at Jason's expression and he knew it was unanimous. Tonight would be a very special night.

* * * *

The cool air in the playroom brushed her skin and soothed her overheated flesh. She'd been on pins and needles for the last few hours, but Gabe and Jason had finally bid the last guest good night and helped the catering company load up their truck. She'd see everyone at the wedding tomorrow, but tonight belonged to only the three of them.

She reached back and unzipped her dress, purchased just for this occasion. It was the first little black dress she'd ever owned and she'd needed the confidence it gave her tonight, but now it was simply in the way. She shrugged it off and hung it from a hook on the wall. She warred over whether she should also remove her black lace bra and panties and her black high heels, but it seemed naughty and decadent to leave them on.

She perused the toys on the walls and shelves, her arousal hitching higher as she took in the selection of butt plugs, floggers, nipple clamps, paddles, and a few things she couldn't identify. She'd read about things like this in some of Sadie's smutty books but tonight she was really going to get to experience it. There wasn't a smidgen of fear inside her, only anticipation. She trusted her men completely. She knew they would take care of her, keeping her from any harm.

She turned on her heel at the sound of their footsteps approaching. A zing ran through her body and her heart rate started to accelerate, galloping like a horse at the Kentucky Derby. They looked handsome and sexy in their suit and ties and she smiled, fantasizing about stripping those clothes from their yummy bodies to explore what was underneath.

Gabe shrugged off his jacket and tossed it on a sofa in the corner. "I like the look, babe. Sexy, black lingerie looks good on you."

Jason was pulling off his jacket and tie as well. "Personally, I think she looks best completely naked. But, you can keep the heels on, sunshine." Jason waggled his eyebrows. If he'd had a mustache, she was sure he would have twirled it with an evil grin.

She stuck her tongue out. "Lech. Aren't you supposed to be teaching me to submit or something?"

Gabe rolled his eyes. "You're no submissive, that's for sure. It doesn't mean we can't play and have some kinky fun though."

Sami stuck out her lower lip. "I want you to teach me to submit."

Gabe sighed and crossed his muscular arms across his chest, straining the fabric of his button down shirt. "The first lesson of submission is the Dominant is in charge. He makes the decisions and controls what happens."

"That sounds sucky. All the decisions?"

Gabe scraped a hand down his face. "All of them, except whether to use your safe word. It takes a strong, confident woman to submit. Trust and honesty is key. Still interested?"

Sami took her time, tapping her chin. "I am. I want to try this."

Jason shook his head. "You don't try submission. You do it."

"Okay, I want to do this, then. Where do we start?"

Jason popped open the buttons on his shirt, revealing his tan chest. "We start with some rules. Rule number one, you do not have permission to speak. If you speak without permission, you will be punished."

"That doesn't seem fair." If she was quiet, how would they know they'd done something she liked or didn't like? It sounded like a bunch of male chauvinist crap.

Jason looked at Gabe. "I think you should run the show. I'm not sure I've had enough lessons for this."

"I doubt anyone has, but I think we first need to get her in the right frame of mind. Kneel, Samantha."

When she didn't respond, he placed his hand on top of her head and spoke again, the deep timbre of his voice sending shimmers of heat through her body.

"Kneel, Samantha. Obey now."

She dropped to her knees instinctively. He'd gone into a commanding mode and damn if her body didn't want to do as he bade. She peeked up at him through her lashes, his face a mask of concentration.

"That's better. Thank you. I want you to put your hands behind your back, lacing your fingers together and leave them there. You can rest your bottom on your heels, if you like."

She moved into position and relaxed. This wasn't so hard.

"You will address us both as 'Sir.' You speak only when spoken to. Your only replies are 'Yes, Sir' and 'No, Sir.' If you need to

speak, you politely ask for permission to do so. Do you understand?"
He was circling her, invading her personal space and she actually
started to feel submissive to him, wanting to please them both more
than she wanted something for herself.

"Um, yes, Sir?"

Gabe nodded and started to strip off his shirt and suit pants.
"Excellent. I think we'll start out with something easy. Samantha,
suck Jason's cock."

Jason had already stripped down to his boxers and she reached for
him but he caught her hands. "Did Gabe tell you to move your hands?
Put them back, Sami."

She reluctantly put her hands back behind her. She'd wanted to
feel his cock underneath her fingers. The velvety skin, the steel
hardness underneath. She loved the way it pulsed in her hand, hot and
ready. Instead, he pushed his boxers down and fed her his cock with
his hand, controlling how much she was able to pull into her mouth.

"Easy, sunshine. I control this, you don't. You accept what we
give you, nothing more."

She fought her instinct to grab his cock and suck it down her
throat until she choked. She allowed him to fuck her face, shallowly
at first, then deeper and faster. His fingers tangled in her hair tightly,
holding her exactly where he wanted her. The soft bite of pain and the
feeling of being under his control sent her arousal into the
stratosphere. Heat swept through her veins and honey dripped from
her pussy, down her thighs. She pressed them together to ease the
ache in her clit and cunt.

Jason noticed her movement and shook his head, wedging his foot
in between her knees. "Uh-uh, no cheating. Spread those thighs for
me."

She would have cursed if her mouth hadn't been full. She pushed
her knees apart and suddenly realized this was submission. It was
about what Jason and Gabe wanted, not what she thought she needed.
Her pussy clenched with need and she sucked on his cock harder and

deeper until he groaned his pleasure.

"That's it. Suck him good, Samantha and you'll get a reward."

She wasn't sure what the reward was but she knew she wanted it. She bobbed her head up and down, taking him as far down her throat as she could. She knew she'd succeeded when his fingers tightened painfully in her hair and curse words fell from his lips.

"Fuck, fuck, fuck. Shit, fuck, I'm gonna blow." Hot jets of cum filled her mouth and she swallowed frantically to keep up. He pulled from her mouth and she sat back on her heels waiting for her next command.

"Fuck, her mouth is dangerous. She's so fucking good at sucking my cock."

Gabe chuckled. "Get her and you a drink of something cool. The night's barely begun."

Her stomach fluttered at the promise in his words. She felt his hand under her elbow helping her to her feet. He swept his arm indicating the toys and implements on the walls and shelves.

"Is there anything you want to try? I'll give you the opportunity to choose a few things as a reward for being a good sub."

Sami stepped forward eagerly just as Jason pressed a cold bottle of water into her hand. She drank thirstily as she shopped for kink, fully aware Gabe and Jason watched her every move and expression. Her gaze landed on a pair of nipple clamps and she scooped them up for Gabe's approval. He smiled and nodded at her selection.

"Excellent choice. Anything else?"

Her fingers caressed the leather handle of a crop. "How about this?"

Gabe pulled it from its hook on the wall. "It's a medium impact. I can work with this."

She walked a few more steps and let her hand trail down the long strands of a flogger. They felt soft against her skin and she turned to Gabe with a hopeful expression. "This one."

He shook his head. "That's a heavier impact. You need to work up to it, babe. How about this one instead? I promise you'll love how it feels."

He moved her hand to a flogger and she grasped the strands, letting them fall through her fingers. She lingered over them as her mind anticipated what they would feel like on her bare skin.

She nodded wordlessly and he pulled it down from the wall. He reached onto a shelf and grabbed a large purple vibe with a clit stimulator.

"You got to choose, this is my selection. Jason, do you want to make a choice?"

Jason grinned and pulled something off the shelf, holding it up for her to see. "A cock ring, sunshine. A vibrating cock ring, to be exact. This is going to drive you crazy when I'm fucking you."

It most certainly would. His cock alone was enough to make her forget her own name but add in vibrations and she was a goner.

Gabe pointed to her. "Strip." Her clothes almost fell off from the sound of his deep, commanding tone alone. She stripped her bra and panties and kicked off her shoes. Jason led her to the St. Andrew's cross but turned her toward him when she thought he would press her back on it. He bent and sucked a nipple into his mouth and she couldn't hold back a tortured moan as his tongue and teeth worried the nub until it was hard and standing at attention. He repeated the process on the other side then stood back in satisfaction.

"She's ready for the clamps."

Gabe's callused fingers brushed her sensitive skin as he placed the tweezer clamp on her nipple and tightened until she winced slightly. She raised her hands to remove it, the burning almost unbearable, when the pain turned into something much more delicious. It was as if there was a string from her nipple directly connected to her clit and her body shook with the power of her arousal. Gabe watched her closely as he attached the second clamp, but this time she knew the pain would turn to pleasure and simply waited for the morphing to complete. She sighed as her body relaxed, the pressure on her breasts never ceasing.

"Good girl. That's my good girl," Gabe praised. "Let's get you on the cross."

She'd been fantasizing about this but nothing prepared her for how it felt as Jason and Gabe, one on each side of her, pressed her front into the cross. They lifted her arms and attached them but kneeling down, widening her legs, and attaching them as well. She tugged against her restraints but she was held firmly. The cool, smooth wood was in contrast to her heated, tumbled thoughts and she let her forehead fall forward against the cement wall. She concentrated on her breathing as she heard her men walking behind her, then the brush of soft strands against her overheated flesh.

"Just relax, sunshine. Let your mind turn off and wander free." It was Jason's voice in her ear, his warm breath on the curve of her neck. They'd barely even done anything to her and she could feel her honey dripping down her thighs and her arousal tightening in her belly with every caress. Their hands rubbed her skin, touching, seeking and making her crazy with want. She cried out in abandonment as they pulled their hands away but they replaced them with the soft, long fingers of the flogger. It swished over her back, bottom, and thighs, then up to tickle her neck and shoulders.

Back and forth it moved until the strands suddenly came down with a soft thud on her bottom. It wasn't enough to hurt her and she eagerly welcomed the sensation all over her body. It felt like a really great massage and by the time the strokes became slightly harder she was arching into them, her skin flushed from the contact.

"Let's change things up and see if you like this as much." Gabe this time. She didn't know what he was talking about but she didn't have time to ask. She heard a whistle through the air then the sting of the crop as it drew a line of heat across her ass cheeks. She was going to tell him off but then the crop came down again, and then one more time.

"I think three is enough. You can tell me if you liked it later."

She was incapable of speech. The heat from her bottom had flown straight to her cunt and she needed something in it badly. She opened her mouth to beg for cock, but only a moan escaped. Gabe patted her sore bottom.

"Do you need to come, little sub? I know what you need."

She was panting, her body covered with sweat when she heard the sound of the vibe and felt the press against her soaked pussy. She was so wet it slid in easily, the rabbit ears snug against her clit, her cunt filled. It took mere moments before her first orgasm hit her, hard and fast. Her knees would have given out if she hadn't been restrained and she screamed as a second wave, stronger than the first took over her body. She gave herself over to the pleasure, letting it have its way. Her breathing was ragged and her head spinning when she came back to earth. Both Jason and Gabe were holding her and telling her how beautiful and wonderful she was. Her head lolled back onto Jason's chest.

"I need a cock."

Jason laughed. "So much for the submissive portion of the evening." He reached up and took off her restraints, before bending down and releasing her ankles. She sagged against him as he swung her up in his arms and carried her over to a large four-poster bed in the corner of the room laying her gently on the silky sheets.

With a hot man stretched out on either side of her, they kissed and licked every square inch of her body until she consumed by the flames they'd fanned. She cried out as their tongues played between her legs, Jason licking her clit and Gabe tongue-fucking her hole. When she didn't think she could take anymore they kissed their way back up, tugging on the nipple clamps as they journeyed to the hollow of her neck and the curve of her shoulder.

Gabe had shucked his boxers and rolled on a condom. He shifted so his weight was on top of her, lifting her legs and wrapping them around his waist. The head of his cock pressed against her for entry and she lifted her hips to accommodate him. He thrust in hard and deep but barely paused, starting a fast and hard rhythm that had her on the edge of orgasm quickly.

Their breathing ragged, their skin hot, Gabe rode her cunt mercilessly. He found the spot that drove her insane and never let up until she screamed his name as her climax spiraled out of control. The room seemed to spin and the lights danced in front of her eyes. The feeling washed over her again and again until she was wrung out, her hands gripping Gabe's shoulders. He felt like sanity and she kissed everywhere she could reach as he hit his own pinnacle. She watched fascinated as he climaxed, his cock jerking inside of her, his face contorted with passion.

When he slumped over her she stroked his back and let their bodies return to some semblance of normal. He levered himself up with a groan and pulled from her sensitive flesh with a grimace. Jason was there with more cool water and she drink gratefully from the bottle he placed on her dry lips.

It appeared Jason was content to let her rest but she needed both her men tonight. She reached for him, pulling his naked body on top of hers. She loved this position when they made love. It never ceased to make her feel small and delicate. When she looked up, their muscular torsos beckoned to her greedy fingers and she allowed herself the luxury of exploring the hard ridges and curves under her palms.

At some point, he'd stripped off his boxers and donned a condom and the cock ring. He handed her the wireless control.

"You can control the vibration. A little or a lot. Whatever you want, sunshine."

She could press the buttons with one hand and she pushed the top button experimentally, immediately jumping as the ring came to life against her hip. She giggled and turned it off before beckoning to Jason.

"I think I have this figured out."

As hard as Gabe had fucked her, Jason was determined to do the opposite. He took his time, slowly thrusting in and out, looking her directly in the eye, and watching which angles gave her the most pleasure. When he found her sweet spot, he grinned and began the inexorable slide over it again and again until she thought she would explode.

She pressed the top button and the vibrations against her clit with every thrust placed her at the edge of a cliff, about to go over. Jason never sped up his leisurely pace, driving them both out of their minds. He was the epitome of the patient male and tonight he was showing her exactly what that meant. She dug her nails into his back to urge him to go faster, but he simply hooked his arms under her thighs and lifted her legs higher and wider so the ring hit more directly on her clit.

Before she could press the off button to drag out the sensations, her climax hit her. She bit into his shoulder riding the relentless waves, almost painful in their intensity. He groaned into her ear and she felt the heat in her cunt as he came, his body tense and stiff. Eventually, they both relaxed, their bodies curled together until Jason left the bed to take care of the condom.

Both men cuddled her close until she found her eyes getting heavy and she slipped into a dreamless sleep. When she awoke, she was alone but she could hear her men's soft voices not far away. She sat up in bed, ready to make a decision that could change all three of their lives forever. They'd wasted too much time apart. They needed to be together. Forever.

She was going to call to them but they returned with a tray of food she knew was leftovers from the party earlier. Her men didn't make cocktail meatballs and parmesan chicken.

"We thought you might be hungry." Gabe set the tray on the bed wearing nothing but a smile.

Jason popped a meatball into his mouth. "I know I am. We worked up an appetite."

Sami didn't answer and her men exchanged a concerned look. She licked her dry lips and screwed up her courage for the second time that evening. "The thing is, I've been thinking."

"About food?" Jason teased.

She swallowed. "No, about us. And you know, the future."

Gabe leaned on his elbow. "The future? How far in the future? Tomorrow? Next week? Or further?"

"Further. The thing is…" She wrung her hands together. "Gran's going to expect us to get married."

She sure as hell hadn't meant to blurt that out. She didn't want to guilt them into marrying her for her grandmother's sake.

Gabe nodded solemnly. "You're right, she will. What do you think we should do about it?"

"I think we should get married."

Jason rubbed his chin. "Will that be enough? Maybe we should have two or three kids? I bet she'd like grandkids."

She was getting a warm feeling in her heart. She could also see smiles on their faces they were trying to hide. She smacked Gabe on the arm.

"You could have asked me, you know. The girl isn't supposed to have to do the asking."

Jason chuckled. "Sunshine, we were terrified of asking. We didn't know if you wanted forever."

"Well, I do," Sami said. "I really do."

Gabe brushed the hair off her face. "We do, too. So, we're getting married then. Just for Gran's sake, of course."

"Of course," Sami echoed. She'd never felt more full of love and happiness than she did at this moment. These men were everything to her. Her whole world.

Jason lifted a meatball to her lips with a smile. "We should probably do it as soon as possible. Because that would make Gran happy."

Her men were grinning now. "Do you think we could get a Justice of the Peace to marry us tonight?"

Gabe shook his head. "How about we grab the first plane to Vegas on Sunday and get married there. We can get married by an Elvis impersonator. Gran always loved Elvis."

Sami clapped her hands, already picturing her wedding. "Gran's going to be so excited."

Jason laughed. "But not surprised. After all, she told us to ensnare you with amazing sex."

Thank goodness for Gran. She'd known what Sami needed even when everything seemed lost and dark. Her men would always want to take care of her and Sami knew there would be times she would have to push back. She would have to stand on her own two feet.

She knew she could do it. She'd faced her greatest fear and come out the other side. She had her whole life ahead of her.

Scratch that. They had their whole lives ahead of them. Together forever in Plenty.

Sami sent a prayer of thank you heavenward for this wonderful second chance. Her second chance with the first, and last, men she'd ever love.

THE END

WWW.LARAVALENTINE.NET

ABOUT THE AUTHOR

I've been a dreamer my entire life. So, it was only natural to start writing down some of those stories that I have been dreaming about.

Being the hopeless romantic that I am, I fall in love with all of my characters. They are perfectly imperfect with the hopes, dreams, desires, and flaws that we all have. I want them to overcome obstacles and fear to get to their happily ever after. We all should. Everyone deserves their very own sexy, happily ever after.

I grew up in the cold but beautiful plains of Illinois. I now live in central Florida with my handsome husband, who's a real, native Floridian, and my son whom I have dubbed "Louis the Sun King." They claim to be supportive of all the time I spend on my laptop, but they may simply be resigned to my need to write.

When I am not working at my conservative day job or writing furiously, I enjoy relaxing with my family or curling up with a good book.

For all titles by Lara Valentine, please visit
www.bookstrand.com/lara-valentine

Siren Publishing, Inc.
www.SirenPublishing.com